Praise for *Normal Vision?*

Normal Vision? is the fourth book in the *Normal?* series. These books fall into the humanist style. I believe most humanist authors seek to elucidate the societal and personal injustices of their times. While the *Normal?* series mentions many contemporary societal and personal injustices the various characters have faced, or are currently facing, the focus is much more on the universal solution to, just about, all injustices—that being love.

In each of the individual books of the *Normal?* series, Stephen Mulrooney's stories not only bring the reader through some of the most basic and universal struggles of individual, familial, and societal life, his characters transport the reader to the answers and solutions to each of these struggles in their expressions of awareness, wisdom, open-mindedness, acceptance, mutual support, community, caring, charity, relationship, and love.

Once again, in *Normal Vision?* Stephen Mulrooney introduces the reader to new characters with their own individual and yet universal struggles. And just as in the past, with each new character, with their own individual "flaw", Stephen Mulrooney shows us the "flaw" is but a shadow cast upon the character by others, or society in general. As Victor Hugo stated in Les Misérables, "The guilty one is not the person who has committed the sin, but the person who has created the shadow."

Just as in all the past books of the *Normal?* series, here in *Normal Vision?* Stephen Mulrooney reminds us of our own missed opportunities to see or do better, or more in our own lives. And then he provides for us new perspectives, new solutions to complex struggles and problems, and most importantly, new paradigms for us to consider and adopt, just as easy as every new member of the extended Poole-Hall family.

Jerome Van Wert, Publisher
Busterfly LLC

Busterfly

a small, personal, fun-loving publishing company

NORMAL VISION?

STEPHEN J. MULROONEY

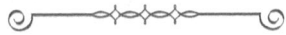

Busterfly
Kansas City, Missouri

Busterfly

Kansas City, Missouri

First Busterfly edition 2025

Busterfly and Busterfly logo are trademarks of Busterfly LLC

Printed in the United States of America

ISBN: 978-1-966476-03-0 (Paperback)
978-1-966476-04-7 (eBook)

Dedication

Normal Vision?, like *Normal?*, *Normal Too?* and *Normal Curve?* that preceded it, is dedicated to the most important person in my life, and the most important person behind these books.

Jerome Van Wert is the chief editor and publisher of this book. I am also fortunate enough to say that he is my husband, and the inspiration for all the love that you'll find throughout the story you're about to read. Could there possibly be a better muse?

As such, *Normal Vision?* is *our* book. Without him, it would still just be a vision. And, as I mentioned in the previous books, as the publisher of my books, every page of every story passes carefully through his loving hands before going to print. He meticulously oversees the edits of every page of the book, designs the cover, chooses the best artist, and picks the perfect book designer. He protects and carefully guides each book through the dozens of steps of the publishing process until he is satisfied that the books are a thing of beauty. They couldn't possibly be in better hands, and they would've never reached your hands without him.

Jerome's love, dedication, and passion make everything in my life possible. This book is but a small sample. To paraphrase the song by The Police, every little thing he does is magic. I believe in magic because I believe in him.

Acknowledgements

There are so many people to thank for their assistance in bringing this book to light. Their input and expertise have been invaluable, and I'm sure you'll find their hard work has helped transform this story into a beautiful work of art.

First, and foremost, I want to thank my publisher, Busterfly, and in particular, Jerome Van Wert, for his expertise as chief editor and publisher of this book, and for his careful selection of the many talented hands it passed through before reaching yours.

I would also like to thank Dr. Camille Cardenas for her reviews and recommendations.

Finally, no book is complete without a great book designer. Through the entire *Normal?* series, we are fortunate to have the best. Clark Kenyon at Camp Pope Publishing is our book designer. You'll find his expertise on every single page. We can't imagine publishing a book without passing it through his skillful hands.

Thank you, Clark, for all the beauty you create.

Andrew Batcheller

We would particularly like to make a special acknowledgement of our dear friend and incredible artist, Andrew Batcheller. Once again, we are extremely fortunate to have an amazing work of art, by this award-winning artist, adorn the cover of our book, *Normal Vision?*. Andrew's paintings are included in many national and international collections. So, to have Andrew Batcheller paint what became the cover art for this book is a great honor.

Andrew Batcheller is a former Kansas City, Missouri, native who has called Joplin, Missouri, his home for more than a decade. Andrew classifies his work as "portraiture" using birds and animals as analogies for the human condition. The emotional quality of his work evokes thoughtful contemplation of our own human drama, and in this case, the human drama found within the covers of this book.

To view other works by Andrew Batcheller, go to
www.andrewbatcheller.com

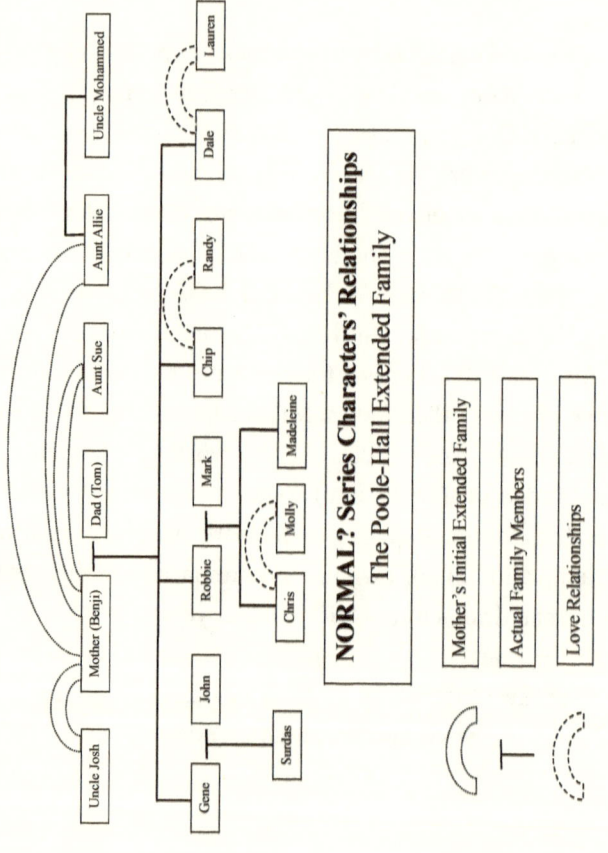

NORMAL? Series Characters' Relationships
The Poole-Hall Extended Family

Mother's Initial Extended Family

Actual Family Members

Love Relationships

Prologue

Our son Surdas was born blind. But that never stopped him from having better-than-normal vision.

Mother, whose quotes have always been insightful, says, "Foresight is the best substitute for sight. It allows you to see something that everyone else is blind to, and to envision something that no one else has ever seen. When it comes to vision, the eyes do not always have it."

A person with foresight has the unique ability to think and plan for the future with imagination and wisdom. We call these people visionaries, because they have the foresight to see what is invisible to everyone else and bring it into reality. They see things as they can be. They see things as they should be, not just the way they are. Their visions are the building blocks of the future.

Mother says, "A visionary takes a set of Legos and turns it into a time machine. What the world does not see, the builder has already envisioned. Superman may be able to see through things, but a person with vision will see things through."

Mother has inspired our entire extended family to always see things through. In doing so, he has given us better-than-normal vision.

Surdas is in every sense of the word a visionary. He believes his blindness gives him insights that sighted people often don't recognize. It allows his imagination to run wild, unfettered by the weight of how things appear when they become too familiar. It allows his other senses to more than compensate for the one he is missing. It allows him to perceive things from a new perspective. He has vision where others merely have sight. From the moment we first laid eyes on him, he taught us the difference between having sight and having vision. And, in doing so, he has opened our eyes in more ways than one.

Mother believes that people with sight, but who lack vision, lead normal lives, because they are blind to the magic in the world. But Surdas's life is anything but normal. Surdas has vision beyond sight. Life without vision is merely living. It is a place where dreams and fantasies come to die. Life with vision is creating. It is a place where dreams and fantasies come to life.

Surdas intends to lead his life as a creator … a builder of dreams … a life-giver to possibilities. He intends for all his dreams and fantasies to come to life. Surdas doesn't need a mirror to see who and what he is. He sees it within.

One

"Why do you suppose people speak louder when they learn that I am blind?" our son Surdas asked John and me laughingly on his first day of high school. "A blind person could go deaf trying to have a conversation with someone who can see. I even think some of the kids at school were using hand gestures and sign language to further emphasize what they were saying."

"People often overcompensate for things they don't understand, Buddy," John replied. "It's like how Bapu Gene's eyes glaze over when anything even remotely connected to electronics, hunting, or cars is mentioned. You don't have to see it to imagine his eyes glazing in his absolute silence."

Surdas couldn't help but laugh at the thought of my eyes glazing over. "Don't worry Bapu Gene," he said tenderly through the laughter, "I'm mostly with you on that one, especially since I don't think I'm going to be shooting any guns or driving any cars anytime soon. And as far as electronics are concerned, I think I may have even plugged my cell phone charger into the cat by accident. Now all I get is catcalls."

I must admit that I appreciated his lighthearted defense as I rubbed his head and asked him how his first day of school went.

"It was pretty cool," he smiled. "There's even another gay kid named Cayenne, who is a little older than me, and who insisted on taking me around to all my classes. I think we're going to be friends."

"Cayenne?" John asked. "Sounds spicy!"

"He thinks he's pretty hot, but I actually think he's pretty cool," Surdas laughed. "He also waited with me for the bus to come home. He said he'll be there tomorrow to help guide me around again. But you guys already knew that—didn't you Bapu Gene?"

"What do you mean, Buddy?" I asked, obviously trying to conceal that I knew what he meant.

"You shouldn't wear the cologne I gave you for your birthday if you're going to spy on me," he giggled. "Why do you think I chose such a strong scent? I could practically sniff out every move you made. I could even tell when you hid around the corner of the school building, even though I obviously wouldn't be able to see you if you didn't."

"Very sneaky," I admitted. "But how do you know it wasn't Bapu John?"

"I bought a different scent for each spy, and you guys

are too sentimental not to wear the one I got specifically for you."

"Extremely devious, Mr. Bond," I laughed. "But I wasn't really spying. I just wanted to make sure everything went well for you on your first day.

"Ok! Maybe on second thought that is spying," I admitted. "But it's the right of every parent to spy on their child. As a matter of fact, just to make sure, we even had it included in the adoption papers. That's why we didn't give you a braille copy of them."

"Good one!" he chuckled. "Is there anything else you're keeping from my fingertips?"

"Nothing I can think of offhand," I jokingly replied. "Except that tomorrow was supposed to be Bapu John's turn."

"Oh well! I guess my hands are tied," he laughed. "Just know that I really am fully capable of making the transition from homeschool to mainstream smoothly on my own. And having said that, I would have been extremely disappointed if one of you wasn't spying on me in the beginning. That's one of the reasons I picked you guys."

"Oh! Now you picked us," John chimed in.

"Not just now," he smiled, "I picked you from the very moment you first laid eyes on me. It just took you a while to see what I envisioned."

"To think," John mused at the idea, "if it wasn't for all your handy work, we could have wound up with a normal teenager."

"I know," he laughed. "You got lucky that way. Just like

I was lucky enough not to wind up with normal parents. Besides, can you imagine the difficulty a normal child would have in this family?"

Two

The next morning, as he promised, Cayenne was waiting for Surdas when he got off the bus. As they walked toward their first class, Cayenne warned him that, as much as he'd like to be friends, Surdas should be aware that any sort of long-term friendship between them could be a problem.

"Why?" Surdas asked seriously, somewhat hurt at the thought. "Is it because I'm blind?"

"Don't be silly," Cayenne laughed. "You may be noticeably blind, but I'm far more noticeably black, Hispanic, and gay. That's a victim trifecta. My accent and taste in clothing are a little too Shakira femme for most bully palates to swallow. That usually adds up to a fair-sized target on the only game in town.

"No offense, but being blind, you probably have enough problems without adding me to the list. Bullies don't discriminate in how they discriminate. Their aim is often off mark, and when you're anywhere around a bulls-eye, you're bound to get hit."

"Before we discuss problems with this friendship," Surdas smiled, "let's sit down outside and talk about potential targets and easy marks. I have a long list of 'Of Alls' I need to run off to you that are not only going to change your mind, but they're also going to blow it.

"First of all, blind people are no less blind to bullies when it comes to bullseyes. The easier the target the more confident they become in marking their mark. There is never any courage to a bully's offense. They only become offensive when they spot a weakness in your defense. I know that well. I was bullied for being blind in a group home before I was adopted. They were able to knock me down, but I never allowed them to get me down. So, being bullied, being a target, is not new to me and doesn't scare me."

"You're adopted?" Cayenne interrupted. "I never met anyone who was adopted. That's so cool! Someone didn't just get stuck with you—they actually picked you. You were wanted. You're so lucky! I was never really wanted. That's how I wound up being raised by my grandmother who never really wanted me either."

"Hey! Hello! I'm working on a list here, Pepper Boy," Surdas grinned, "one story at a time."

"Pepper boy?" Cayenne laughed. "I like the tag! Please continue."

"Second of all, my adopted parents, Bapu Gene and Bapu John are gay."

"No way! That's unbelievably cool! I never met anyone with gay parents either. That's so cool, it's frozen. But what's with the whole *Baba Looey* thing? Is that another tag like baba ghanoush, or something?"

"Bapu is an endearing Hindi term for father. In case you haven't noticed, I'm Indian."

"I guess that explains the great tan," Cayenne laughed. "All I noticed was that you were kind of cute and liked to wear those cool rose-colored sunglasses."

"Hey! Don't be spreading flirt all over my list. I'm just getting started, and you're making me forget which 'Of All' I'm working on. We're still on the first page.

"Third through at least fourteenth of all, my adopted grandparents, great-aunts, aunt, and uncles are all gay. One of my grandparents and both great-aunts were former star performers in a famous drag club. And the rest of the family that isn't gay is possibly even more diverse, since it includes two great-uncles, one a rabbi and the other a Sufi master; and two cousins, one a straight jock and the other a girl who is still too young to know if she is diverse in any other way than just being a girl.

"And last, and certainly not least of all, I've been carrying a not-so-secret crush on my best friend, soul mate, and adopted cousin, Chris, the straight jock, for at least four years. So, technically, I'm pretty sure that also makes me gay, even if I've never had the experience.

"So, taking all that into consideration, I think my full house beats your three of a kind. And maybe you should be a little more concerned about any fallout from a friendship with me, than I should be with you."

Cayenne just sat there in what must have been wide-eyed in amazement for a few minutes, not saying a word. Finally, Surdas interrupted the silence by asking if his revelations had scared him away.

"What are you kidding me?" he gushed in amazement. "I'm trying to figure out how to run away and join the Surdas Circus. It seems the only thing you guys don't have is elephants. You don't have elephants, do you?"

"Not that I've seen," Surdas joked. "But you never know what you're going to find when you get home. So, who knows?"

"So how do I join?" Cayenne asked rather seriously.

"The membership requirements aren't that strict," Surdas laughed. "You can still keep your family and come over and meet the rest of the show this weekend if you'd like. I'm sure Mother would be thrilled to host my new friend under the big tent."

"Wait!" Cayenne exclaimed. "I thought you had two fathers. You didn't mention anything about a mother."

"Sure I did," he smiled. "Mother is one of my grandfathers. He was the featured star of the drag show that included my two great-aunts, who technically are more like great-uncles, but only technically.

"Mother has always taken care of everyone, so everyone calls him Mother. And because of that, everyone calls his husband, my other grandfather, Dad. It's one of the reasons I don't call my parents that. Titles can get pretty confusing when you're bending more than genders."

"If this gets any more exciting, I'm going to pee in my pants," Cayenne laughed.

"Then you'd better be wearing *Depends*, Pee Brain," Surdas chuckled. "The excitement hasn't even begun yet. I'll hobnob with my fellow wizards and arrange a trip to Emerald City for you. You're about to discover a rainbow of welcomes in the Merry Old Land of Odds."

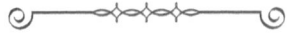

Three

Surdas knew that John and I would be thrilled to learn that he had found a new friend so quickly. With his best friend Chris away at Georgetown University on a soccer scholarship, and Chris's girlfriend Molly away at MIT on an academic one, his social activities for the past two years mostly revolved around playing with Chris's little sister Madeleine when Robbie and Mark were in town, conversations with older family members, and nightly Zoom conversations with Chris.

Although Zooming was a bit less satisfying for Surdas than for Chris, since Surdas obviously couldn't see Chris, the sessions were always the highlight of Surdas's day. The sound of Chris's voice would never fail to cheer Surdas up, and he would often fall asleep hugging his tablet, with a huge grin on his face after the call.

If that sounds at all bleak, it absolutely wasn't. Everyone in our amazing family did their best to bridge the gap in distance between Chris and Surdas. They included him in many of their daily activities, and they brought him to as many of Chris's soccer games at Georgetown as possible.

And Chris, who to Surdas's way of thinking is more than just amazing, did an exceptional job of dividing between Surdas and his girlfriend Molly, what little break time from school he had, even to the point of including Surdas on some of his infrequent dates with Molly.

Still, for the most part, at fourteen, Surdas was a teenager deprived of much of the exciting stimulus of being a teenager. So, the mainstreaming into public school and the thrill of his newfound friendship with Cayenne appeared to be just the cluster balm he needed.

Four

Meanwhile, there didn't appear to be any balms going off for Robbie in Albany. On each of his brief visits home, everyone could tell he was trying too hard to be Robbie, to actually be Robbie. As close as he and I are, even I couldn't get him to open up as to what was troubling him.

Mark confided that everything was a lot more complicated in the political world than they expected. The governor, who was apparently wary of Robbie's popularity, kept Robbie at a distance. The legislature had its own agenda and wasn't really interested in any of his potential social projects. And his political party wanted him to remain squeaky clean and avoid any type of political controversy, because the governor was ill and probably wouldn't run for a second term. There was an excellent chance that if Robbie didn't make any waves, in less than two years, the governorship would be his.

Robbie accepted the offer of lieutenant governor because he saw it as a way to make a change. The image he envisioned turned out to be a mirage, an illusion. The insights that he set his sight on were blindfolded, and as such, he couldn't see a way out of his predicament.

Five

Mother was more than thrilled to host Surdas's new friend, Cayenne, for dinner and to meet the family the following weekend. Chris was, of course, away at college, and Robbie, Mark, and Madeleine were back in Albany attending a governor's function for visiting dignitaries. Mother, however, had no trouble gathering what was left of the clan for the function.

Mother's invitations are always a no-brainer. His dinners are culinary experiences that no one in their right mind would resist. There is magic in everything Mother does, so once you've fallen under one of his gastronomical spells, you're enchanted for life.

Surdas had hoped to gently ease Cayenne into the family gathering by first introducing him to John and me, then Mother and Dad, then Uncle Mohammed and Uncle Josh, then Dale and her girlfriend Lauren, and Chip and his boyfriend Randy, and then ease his way up to the great-aunts. But it should come as no surprise to anyone who knows my family, that it was the killer aunts, Aunt Sue and Aunt Allie, in full drag regalia and sprinting in four-heeled-drive, who greeted them first.

"Why didn't anybody tell me that your little friend was one of those *For Colored Girls …* type of girls?" Aunt Sue began the somewhat awkward greeting before Surdas had a chance to introduce Cayenne. "Our gatherings could use a little dose of estrogen."

"I'm not sure what that means," Surdas replied quite perplexed.

"Sorry, Baby! I'm dating myself with the "*For Colored Girls …*" Broadway reference, seeing as no one else seems interested in dating me. What I mean is, you could have told us that you were bringing a beautiful black princess to meet the family. For some reason, everyone seemed to think you were bringing some sort of boy of sorts."

"Cayenne is some sort of boy of sorts, Auntie," Surdas blurted, before realizing how that sounded. "I mean he *is* a boy. And I have to admit, for some reason, I never noticed what color he was."

"That's probably because you're blind, Sweetie," Aunt Allie said sincerely.

"Oh how I wish you were just playing dumb, Allie," Aunt Sue scoffed. "You haven't a clue. And if anyone gave you a clue, you still wouldn't have a clue."

"The only Clue I know is a game," Aunt Allie replied honestly, "and you should know by now that I don't play those types of games, especially not Clue."

"Of course not, you've always been clueless. The only

chasm that exists in sarcasm is to be found in your brain," Aunt Sue replied exhaustedly. "Your mind is so ridiculously vacuous, that with every thought you can hear a pun drop."

As Aunt Allie tried to figure out if that was a compliment or a slight, Aunt Sue returned his attention back to Cayenne.

"You're a boy, Princess?" Aunt Sue asked, as kindly as he is wont to ask. "In that case, despite the what-were-you-thinking clothes, the hair-don't, and the hair dye that looks like it did, you have a lot of potential. I love the challenge of making a mold out of something moldy. I should take you under my supernova wing and make you a drag star, or at least a starlet to start.

"We even have a few perfect costumes for you to try on from when I used to be your size, only prettier. It will be my pleasure to share them with you. After all, birds of a feather frock together. And my outfits will knock your frocking socks off.

"Why you're so femme, you would hardly even have to impersonate anyone to do it," he continued. "You make Old Allie and me look like rugby players by comparison. We may even have to butch you up a bit just so people know you're a female impersonator. Do you really still have all your boy parts?"

"Oh My God, Aunt Sue, you did not just ask that," Surdas said in amazement.

"Yes, he did," Aunt Allie responded quickly. "I heard him too. I was shocked. I would never have asked anything like that, even though I was sort of wondering the same thing."

"They're all there," Cayenne responded rather shyly, yet seemingly unshaken by the barrage. "Though sometimes I'm not so sure they should be. That's not to say I don't want them to be there or anything. I just think I'm more often in touch with my feminine side than not."

"See," Aunt Sue said addressing Surdas defensively, "you worried about nothing ... no harm, no foul, Baby. Little Cayenne here is of the same ilk as your old aunties and even has a little extra Charo in him. 'Parts is just parts,' as they say. In the worlds within worlds, what counts is what shows and what doesn't show, and what's inside and what's out. And I can tell that what's inside our little friend here is pure drag stardust. And I'd like to shake off the regular dust and bring it out."

"Really! Do you really think so?" Cayenne asked, obviously already glowing. "Can you teach me how to be a drag star?"

"Pero por supuesto, Baby!" Aunt Sue assured him. "Drag is not exactly Rockette science. Stay long enough in our galaxy and you'll have your own solar system. Creative potential is not written in the stars—it's written by them. And star power is astronomical when you know how to wield it."

"I agree, but can we stick to a common language?" Aunt Allie asked sheepishly. "No habanero Española, if you poor flavor."

"Okaaay," Cayenne answered, trying to straighten out

in his mind if the comment was supposed to be humorous or not.

"Pay no attention to that poor old thing," Aunt Sue snickered. "Old Allie here is a refugee from The Witless Protection Program. None of her senses make any. Her gray matter doesn't matter at all. Just think of her as a lamp that's never been lit."

"Are you really serious about this star-maker stuff?" Cayenne asked, changing the subject while trying to avoid any potential killer aunt stings. "Can you really teach me to be a famous performer like you two and Mother?"

"We're star whores, Baby!" Aunt Sue laughed. "The farce is always with us."

"Don't you mean force?" Cayenne laughed.

"You've got a lot to learn, Star Child," Aunt Sue's voice smiled, "a lot to learn. It's the law of attraction. You have to be an attractive force to be a famous drag performer. You not only have to be alluring, but you also have to spend as much time as possible gravitating in the farce field, if you're going to drag in an audience. Farce is who you are. It's what you do. Farce is the force that drags people into a drag show. A drag show without farce is exactly that—a farce."

"Surdas was right," Cayenne gushed. "This is a fantasy come true. This is just like being in OZ."

"We should think of a drag name for him that's really hot," Aunt Allie said excitedly.

"You mean like Cayenne?" Aunt Sue asked exhaustedly. "His name is Cayenne. I think that's pretty hot."

"Or we could do Pepper," Cayenne chimed in. "Surdas calls me Pepper. And I like the idea of a new name that sounds a bit draggier."

"Pepper ... or maybe Pepper Mill, or Grinder," Aunt Sue added. "Pepper Grinder sounds hot and sexy. I like it."

"Perfect!" Aunt Allie exclaimed, somewhat confused. "Cayenne Pepper it is! And since cayenne is a pepper anyway, that will make it even easier to remember."

"If only there was some way to make your part of the conversation easier to forget," Aunt Sue sighed. "See what I mean, Cayenne Baby. You'll find smarter heads in a cabbage patch. If she wasn't such a fruit, you would swear she was some sort of walking vegetable."

"Well, it's a good thing we're not really in Oz like Cayenne thinks," Aunt Allie replied, as they walked toward Mother's house. "Because, if we were, there'd be a house falling on you right about now. But, think about it, if he really does think this is just like being in Oz, would that make us witches, wizards, or fairies?"

"More like the whores of a different color," Aunt Sue chuckled. "Besides, since we are not only enchanting, and we're trying to help him over the rainbow, why would he think we were witches?"

"Well, I don't need a house to fall on me to answer that," Aunt Allie laughed. "You do like to eat all those munchkins at *Dunkin Donuts*."

"Snap, Girlfriend! That was a good one. Exactly when did you get so clever, all of a sudden?" Aunt Sue asked.

"That's right!" Aunt Allie responded. "All of a sudden is

exactly when I get clever! I may sometimes seem as dumb as a scarecrow, but I've never had any trouble being *Wicked* on demand."

Six

Mother's dinner was ... well one of Mother's dinners. In other words, as fabulous as anything you'd expect in OZ. And Cayenne had a better than Dorothy-in-Emerald City-type welcome from the rest of the family.

John and I offered him an open-door policy anytime he'd like to come visit. Dale and Chip promised to include him in some of the movie and game nights they spend with Surdas. Uncle Josh promised a few stories. Mother and Dad promised many more dinners. Uncle Mohammed promised to teach him how to defend himself. And Aunt Sue and Aunt Allie set up dates for makeovers and drag sessions.

By the time all the getting-to-know-each-others were over, Cayenne was over the rainbow and floated home in a bubble of true magic, somehow knowing that his life would never again be the same.

After Cayenne left, Surdas volunteered to help Mother clean up in the kitchen so that they could talk about his new friend a little further. Mother was just finishing telling him how much he enjoyed Cayenne's company when Dale, who had been uncharacteristically quiet during dinner, came into the kitchen to ask Mother if she could discuss something important with him. Surdas started to excuse himself so that they could have some privacy, but Dale insisted he stay because she always enjoyed his input.

"Lauren and I want to get married," she began quite nervously, "and we want it to be something special. But we also want it to be soon—maybe no more than a week or two away. We know that's not much time, and there is so much to think about, so I'm hoping you can help us sort it all out before it all gets out of sorts."

"You know I live for these things," Mother gushed. "But why the big rush?"

"It may seem a bit old-fashioned considering the circumstances, but we would really like to be married well before the baby is born."

"What?" Mother and Surdas asked rather loudly in unison.

"Lauren is pregnant," she said happily. "We didn't want to say anything until we were sure, and it happened a lot quicker than we expected."

"Wait! What am I missing here?" Mother asked. "You and Lauren are having a baby, and you're both girls, so who's the father?"

"Sounds like Uncle Chip may have had a hand in there," Surdas laughed.

"It wasn't his hand, or any other body part, so to speak,"

Dale responded. "But yes, Chip is the donor, and you're growing up way too fast, young man.

"Lauren and I wanted to start a family, and we figured that there was no better way to have a child that was a part of us both than having my twin as the donor. We just didn't expect it to happen on the first try."

"Well, it *is* Uncle Chip!" Surdas laughed further.

"Hello! What did I say about growing up too fast?" Dale said, with a smile in her voice that somewhat agreed with the statement.

"Do you think your brother will be hands-off enough for you both to be comfortable," Mother asked, sounding a bit worried.

"We already warned him that if he wants to remain Uncle Chip rather than Aunt Chip, his responsibility has already reached its climax," she responded sincerely.

"I bet that made him cringe," Surdas chuckled, and then quickly apologized for still growing up too fast.

"Anyway," Dale continued, "I could really use your advice in sorting a few things out."

"The food and decorations for the reception are already taken care of, Sweetie," Mother said confidently. "The Aunts and I will take care of that. So what else do you need?"

"Actually, I really didn't want you to go through all that trouble. I want you to be able to enjoy the wedding."

"I'll enjoy it more if I know you'll have excellent food and a beautiful setting. So, what else do you need?"

"Mostly some advice on how to keep the whole family

involved so no one's feelings get hurt. We've already decided that Chip will be best man and Molly will be maid of honor, but we would like everyone else in the family to feel a part of it too."

"I have an idea that may help a little," Surdas volunteered, before Mother had a chance to speak. "If you have a multi-denominational ceremony at my dad's chapel, that could take care of Bapu John, Uncle Josh, and Uncle Mohammed, while at the same time having a service that is absolutely beautiful and unique."

"Like I said, I'm glad you're growing up so fast," Dale laughed. "Now what about the rest of the family? I would really like to have everyone involved. They all mean so much to me, in so many different ways, that I want to make sure no one feels left out."

"Well, if you really want to make it more than decidedly gay and stretch the wedding party out a bit," Mother suggested, "you could have your other two brothers as groomsmen and the aunts as bridesmaids. Robbie and Gene will pose stunning figures across from Sue and Allie who will look more like figures that have been stunned."

"I like it. Keep going," Dale implored. "We're getting there."

"Well," Mother continued, "Dad and I could escort you up the aisle and Lauren's parents could escort her. And then, Dad and Lauren's father could give the respective brides away. So, then we're down to Mark, Chris, Surdas, and Madeleine, who could, of course, be flower girl."

"I would do drag if I could be Chris's partner," Surdas not-so-jokingly volunteered.

"Slap yourself on the back of the head for me," Mother replied, "and seriously put that magic brain of yours to work, before I have to drag your drag back to reality."

"OK! If you really want to be different and include everyone," he responded seriously, "Uncle Mark could be another groomsman and little Madeleine a cute little bridesmaid. Then, Chris could be a ringbearer and I could be flower boy. It's already a pretty gay wedding, anyway, so why not go all out? And I'm sure Chris wouldn't mind the ringbearer role since someone has to help guide the flower boy down the aisle."

"You may not believe this, but I absolutely love it," Dale gushed. "And I'm sure Lauren will too. We'll not only include everyone, but we'll also give the other guests something they'll remember for the rest of their lives."

"If you were a girl, I think I'd have to marry you instead," she teased, as she hugged and kissed Surdas.

"Thanks, but if I were a girl, I'd be giving Molly a run for her money with Chris," he laughed.

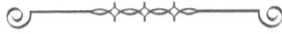

Seven

The following week was probably one of the most amazing weeks in the Poole-Hall extended family history. The entire family pulled together all their resources, and changed all their commitments, to make Dale and Lauren's wish come true, and have their wedding within a week's time.

The aunts helped Mother prepare enough food to feed twice as many guests as the fifty or so family and friends invited, and still have enough left over to send everyone home with gastronomical wedding favors.

John and I hired a staff to serve the food at the wedding reception, so that Mother and the rest of the family could simply enjoy the ceremony and reception, without having to worry about the banquet details.

Chip, Robbie, and Mark arranged for all the flowers and assorted decorations that the aunts would need to adorn the wedding reception tent provided by Uncles Josh and Mohammed.

Lauren's parents provided appropriate limousine transportation for everyone.

And with Dad's assistance, Chris, Molly, and Surdas arranged for music appropriate for all the guests attending—especially the brides. So, as you might expect, there was a healthy dose of k.d. lang, Melissa Etheridge, Tracy Chapman, and Hayley Kiyoko to go along with a few familiar wedding standards, including the *YMCA* song, which is probably the gayest song of all.

To no one's amazement, by the time the wedding eve rolled around, everything, including the decoration of the chapel, was in order. Robbie and Mark were back home with their son Chris, and daughter Madeleine. Molly was back home at her parents' house. So, everyone, including Molly and Lauren's parents, gathered for one of Mother's buffet dinners just outside our home, because no one dared go anywhere near Mother's wedding feast or the aunts' decorations.

Needless to say, the evening was absolutely brilliant with the family all together for the first time in what seemed like ages. The laughter and catch-up conversations lasted until early the next morning.

You might think that everyone would be tired by the time the wedding rolled around the next afternoon, but everyone, including the adults who imbibed a little, looked bright-eyed and bushy-tailed when they arrived at the chapel.

All the groomsmen, Chris, and Surdas wore black tuxedos with white boutonnieres. The best man, Chip, wore a black tuxedo with a red boutonniere. The aunts wore simple beige evening gowns with gold rose corsages and multicolored bouquets. Madeleine wore a beige dress that matched the gowns, with a smaller version of the corsages and bouquets. The maid of honor, Molly, also wore a beige evening gown with a red rose corsage and a multicolored bouquet. John and Uncles Josh and Mohammed all wore white vestments appropriate to their denominations. Dad and Lauren's father also wore black tuxedos with white boutonnieres. Lauren's mother also wore a beige evening gown and a white rose corsage. And Mother wore a white tuxedo with a red rose boutonniere.

All the details were of course relayed to Surdas by Chris, who stood at the back of the chapel with him and the parents of the brides as they waited for the brides to arrive. When they finally did, Chris told Surdas that they were so stunningly beautiful that it would be almost impossible to describe. But then again, it was Chris.

The brides were not in wedding gowns. Instead, they wore elegant gold evening gowns with rainbow-colored roses in their hair and bouquets. There was something almost mystical about their appearance. Chris told Surdas that if they were in a Miss Universe contest, it would have to be a dead heat, because you couldn't possibly choose one above the other.

Dad even commented to Lauren's father, "Are we sure we want to give these two away? We may never see anything this beautiful again."

"We're not giving them away," Lauren's father responded, with a tearful smile in his voice. "We're merely lending them to a happier life. They may belong to each other; but in our hearts, they'll always be ours."

As the brides were escorted down the aisle, without turning around, I could hear the forty, or so, guests in the audience, including Cayenne, catching their breath at the visions of loveliness passing by. Chris and Surdas followed them, somewhat out of turn. But it was okay, because they managed to do it without either of them winding up in anyone's lap. Knowing what clowns they can be when they're together, that alone was unusual and a large plus.

The ceremony itself couldn't have been more stunning. All the words spoken, and passages read by John and Uncle Josh, whom John lovingly referred to as The Best Mensch, and the prayers sung by Uncle Mohammed, whom John called The Bard of Honor, were beautiful and poignant. At times I could hear sniffling, and handkerchiefs being used as the words of love showered over the brides and spilled over the guests. When Dale and Lauren were finally pronounced wife and wife, Surdas said that he knew they had kissed before Chris even told him, by the sounds of applause and happy tears.

After the ceremony was over and the brides made their way out of the chapel, Chris escorted Surdas back up the aisle following the rest of the wedding party. And, miraculously, only the flower basket wound up in someone else's lap. As they left the chapel, the boys received the tail end of the shower of rose petals that had been thrown at the brides, and they were quickly ushered with the rest of us into waiting limousines for the wedding photos and the eventual feast.

Just from Chris's descriptions, Surdas said he could imagine how beautifully spectacular the reception decorations were when we finally arrived back home. And, according to Chris, the only thing besides the brides that could possibly rival them, and surely did, was the banquet that Mother had prepared. If there is a food heaven, we were all transported there.

And speaking of heaven, when Dale and Lauren danced to their wedding theme song, Whitney Houston's version of *I Will Always Love You*, there wasn't a dry eye in the house, as everyone was carried there by the sheer beauty of the way they looked, and looked at each other.

"I know you can't see this," Chris whispered in Surdas's ear as the brides danced and Chris pulled Surdas into this warm, beautiful hug, "But I love you, Bronco ... and it looks the way this feels."

Surdas loves it when Chris calls him Bronco, almost as much as he loves Chris. And this time, it made him cry.

Although it was the brides' special day, it felt like Surdas's special day too. He was surrounded by Chris, Molly, Robbie, Mark, and little Madeleine, all of whom he loved and deeply missed. He had Cayenne by his side for most of the reception. He danced with both brides, both great-aunts, Molly, and even little Madeleine. He received multiple hugs and kisses from all the members of the family, and from Cayenne for inviting him. And he even got a special little nuzzle and kiss to the back of his neck from

Chris, who didn't dance, save a mandatory one with Molly, but held Surdas from behind during one of the more beautiful songs.

Oh, yeah! It was Surdas's special day too.

Eight

It didn't take long for Surdas to discover the type of prejudice Cayenne had warned him about when they first started school. The week after Dale and Lauren's wedding, as he waited by his locker for Cayenne to arrive, he was accosted by one of his classmates, Seth, who had a history of being a bully, and of particularly harassing Cayenne.

"Hey, Stevie Wonder! Where's your little fairy bitch, seeing-eye dog?" Seth sneered, as he poked Surdas against his locker. "Did he leave the little blind mouse waiting in the dark while he went sniffing up someone else's butt?"

Surdas knew the voice, knew the consequences, but he wasn't about to let it go. He had been through this scene too many times in his life to ever let it go again.

"Why don't you just grow up, Seth, and leave Cayenne alone?" Surdas responded angrily. "You're like some stupid little kid that no one likes. So, you try to make up for it by pretending that you're better than someone else.

"The problem is you're not. You're not better than anyone else. And you're not because you're more comfortable acting like an ignoramus than someone who deserves to be liked. As hard as it may seem for someone like you to believe, being a bully just makes you look and sound that much more ignorant. And if you stay on your brainless path, the resulting lack of brain cells will eventually lead to jail cells."

"Eat me, Brownie!" Seth yelled, as he grabbed Surdas's shirt and shoved him against his locker causing him to drop a braille text and laptop.

"You think you're real clever, don't you? I guess the cat only got your eyes, not your tongue, Pussy Boy. Well, maybe you need a lesson. Maybe, instead of Cayenne, you're the real fairy in the fairy tale."

Surdas knew how to defend himself. But he was too dazed by the suddenness of the response that he should have known was coming and couldn't react quickly enough to fend off the attack.

Before he could even think about defending himself with any kind of response, however, Seth's hands released him and he heard this loud thud, followed by a crash at his feet, and Seth's moaning, "What the fuck?"

"Pick everything up and apologize while you're still able to," said a forceful and firm voice that Surdas didn't recognize. "Do it, NOW!"

"Fuck ..." Seth started to say, before slamming against the lockers and hitting the floor again with an even louder thud.

"I was just joking around," Seth responded, obviously

in pain. "What's with all the karate, judo shit, anyway? Are you serious?"

"Jokes are funny," the voice replied. "You're not funny. So, yes, I'm serious. You're a bully, though there's a lot more cow than bull in you, because only a coward would pick on someone at a disadvantage.

"So, you see, chickenshit," the voice continued, "the real funny thing is that the joke is not only on you; it is you. And if you insist on making a joke out of yourself, I can easily be your punch line. And you can bet I will be if I ever catch or hear of you bothering Surdas or his friend again.

"Now, unless the joke needs another punch line, pick everything up while you still have that useless head on your shoulders, apologize, and get out of here."

"Man, I said I was just playing with the guy. What's the big problem?" Seth muttered, as he stood up and brushed himself off.

"Picking on someone because you think they're somehow different, whether it's being gay, or blind, or anything else, is the problem," the voice said firmly. "So, *you're* the big problem. And it's bigger than you think. So don't make me a solution to your problem … because I will solve it."

"OK! I'm sorry!" Seth said, as he carefully handed Surdas's text and laptop back to him. "Everything is cool. We're cool! The laptop is fine. It's in its case and landed on my feet when it fell. So, it's all fine. OK? We're good. I'm just …"

"Gone!" the voice finished the sentence emphatically.

And with that, Seth took off as quickly as he could.

"Thanks!" Surdas said, turning his attention to the voice he still didn't recognize. "I really appreciate the rescue. You know my name. Do we know each other?"

"We haven't actually met yet," the voice responded. "I'm fairly new here, and in the grade above you. My name is Shalom Akbar."

"Shalom Akbar?" Surdas asked, somewhat surprised. "That's quite an impressive name. Does it have a particular significance?"

"It's a combination of two languages whose adherents are often at odds with each other. It means great peace. I think that my parents couldn't live up to the burdens that their Middle Eastern parents placed upon them, so they passed them on to me with the name. They seem to expect me to be some great force for good in the world."

"That sounds pretty heavy. What does that mean for you?" Surdas asked.

"A lot of work and study. I've spent two years studying at a Shinto temple in Japan, three as a Buddhist novice in Thailand, and three more as a disciple of a Hindu guru in India. I've studied with Sikhs, Jains, mystics, and Kabbalists. I know just about every form of spiritual martial arts and meditation ever invented. I've done all of this under my parents' guidance, and I still don't know who I am and what I'm supposed to do in this life. Does that answer your question?" he said sounding a little irritated.

"I'm sorry! I didn't mean to upset you." Surdas responded sheepishly.

"You didn't upset me, Surdas," he said apologetically. "The way I handled Seth did. I'm supposed to be about great peace. I'm supposed to be able to settle things more positively. But when I saw him abusing you, I let my anger get the better of me. It's a problem I have yet to overcome. I'm sure that I could have managed it in a way that would have been better for everyone involved."

"Maybe!" Surdas smiled. "But I'm more than grateful that you handled it for me. I don't have many friends here and I'm literally still feeling my way around. As you can probably imagine, I was a little blindsided by the attack, and I'm quite sure that wouldn't have been my last time dealing with Seth if you hadn't stepped in."

"I'm glad I could help, but it would have been so much better if I had stepped up, rather than stepped in. In any case, I'm glad we finally met. We're kind of in the same boat. I don't really fit in or have many friends either. Actually, since I'm new, and in many ways different from most of the others, I really don't have any friends at all. So, it's nice to meet someone in the same predicament that I can talk to. Do you mind if I walk you to your class?"

"I thought you'd never ask," Surdas grinned. "But how did you know my name?"

"I asked around," he said shyly. "I somehow knew that you were someone I'd like to get to know. Sometimes you get a sense about these things. If you're free later, maybe I can even walk you home, so we can get to know each other better."

"I usually take the bus home," Surdas said with a grin,

"but suddenly I feel like walking. I may not see you after classes, but I'll wait for you anyway."

"You're pretty cool, Surdas," he said as they reached Surdas's class. "I'm glad I finally met you. I'll catch you later."

I don't even know you, or have any idea what you look like, Surdas thought as they parted, *but I think you're pretty hot. You can catch me any time you want.*

Nine

Surdas may have been a bit too effusive in the telling, but he couldn't wait to tell Cayenne about Shalom Akbar after class. He was more than surprised to find Cayenne not only disinterested, but increasingly upset by the recapping of the morning's events. Although he obviously couldn't see his reaction, Surdas could actually feel Cayenne's frowns and growing hostility toward the retelling of the story.

"Is everything OK?" he finally asked, growing uncomfortable with Cayenne's reaction. "You seem somewhat put off by the whole encounter."

"Of course everything's OK," Cayenne snapped uncharacteristically. "Why wouldn't it be? You had your own little gay version of the Prince and the Princess story while I was gone. It sounds absolutely lovely ... like a fairy tale ... a little wet dream come true.

"Everyone deserves their own little 'Once Upon a Time' story once in a while. I'm happy for you. Let's just hope that it doesn't turn out to be one of those Grimm fairy tales where the ending isn't as happy as the princess thought it would be. Let's hope yours ends with, 'and they lived happily ever after.'

"So, you see, it's not a problem at all. It's just that not everyone has the time to listen all the way through to the 'they lived happily ever after' part. So, if I seem a bit off, it's because it's time for me to be so."

"You seem a little more off than usual," Surdas tried to joke. "Did I do or say something to upset you?"

"How could you, Baby? You're perfect! Right? And I'm sure Temple Boy is perfect too—storybook perfect. That's him right … the new boyfriend I see approaching … linen, temple beads, and all? Why even the clothes must be designed by the Dali Lama, or perhaps just Oscar Delhi Rented. What's his name again, Ashram Kabob?"

"What's with you?" Surdas asked, surprised at the apparent attack. "I don't understand. Shalom Akbar is really nice. You'd really like him if you just gave him a chance. And he was defending you as well as me when Seth was being so mean this morning."

"Oh, goodness, where are my manners? Remind me to send him one of those thought-provoking transcendental thank-you messages," Cayenne responded. "You know, something cosmic, or at least cosmetically spiritual. And, since you two are so chummy, why do you call him by his full name instead of his first name?"

"Shalom Akbar is his first name. I don't even know his last name yet. We just met."

"Two first names? Isn't that special! Does he have a personality or face to go with each one of them?"

"Come on Cayenne, stop it!" Surdas pleaded. "Just meet him. You'll like him. Just give him a chance."

"As much as I love a game of Chance, the game board is getting crowded," he mocked. "It will have to be another time. I have no time for games. I'll leave that to you two playmates. It's my move. And I must run."

And so, he did, seconds before Shalom Akbar got there.

"You look upset. Is everything OK?" Shalom Akbar asked, placing his hand on Surdas's shoulder. "Why did your friend run off so quickly? I would have liked to have met him."

"Cayenne's a bit of an enigma," Surdas assured him. "He either had something pressing on his mind, or there was something he absolutely had to do. It's just who he is."

"Whatever it is, he must be someone special if he's your friend."

"Are you flirting with me?" Surdas asked, trying to be coy.

"Not really," Shalom Akbar said seriously. "I don't flirt with anyone because flirting implies some sort of personal or sexual interest that I don't, or at least can't, have right now. It seems to be an important part of every discipline I've studied. I hope you understand that I certainly don't mean to offend or embarrass you in any way. I'm just being truthful.

"I really don't think of myself as a sexual being, neither heterosexual, nor homosexual, nor anything in between for that matter. It is my belief that we are all spiritual beings, and I try to relate to everyone on that level. Every teaching I've been involved with indicates that sex and intimate relationships are impermanent and a distraction on such a path. And so, it is a course that I feel I must follow.

"I hope that you can understand and respect all that I'm telling you and still remain my friend."

"I believe that all friendships are intimate relationships to some degree," Surdas responded, embarrassed and disappointed. "But I respect you for who and what you want to be. And I will be whoever and whatever I need to be, in order to be your friend.

"So, I apologize if I made you uncomfortable. I certainly never meant to. I know we just met but I really like you."

"You didn't make me uncomfortable, Surdas. It is sometimes as confusing for me as I'm sure it is for you. And I really like you too. That's why I want to walk you home. I just thought it better to set things straight, so to speak. As much as I try to practice nonattachment, I wouldn't mind being somewhat attached to a friend while I'm here."

"You have one," Surdas said, not really feeling the whole nonattachment thing himself. "What do you mean by while you're here?"

"I'm staying with my grandmother in town while my parents are in Bhutan. My grandmother needs a little help while she recovers from hip surgery. And I needed some more education credits. So, here I am.

"I'll finish this semester, and my parents will send for me wherever they wind up next. It seems to be the way we spend our lives. My destiny, for now, appears to be that of a spiritual nomad."

"Does all the learning and traveling make you happy?" Surdas asked.

"Let's just say I'm content," he answered sincerely. "I practice contentment. I'm still not sure whether I'm happy or not. I'm not even sure what happiness is when compared to a path you feel you should be following."

"Whatever it means to you," Surdas sincerely responded, "I hope that you find it."

As they walked home, Surdas felt that it was almost as though he was walking home with Chris, only somehow a little softer, a little gentler. With the slightest touch, Shalom Akbar would guide Surdas past any obstacle in his path, and almost nonchalantly mention anything of interest that Surdas obviously couldn't observe. It was everything that he experienced and missed with Chris, and more.

Shalom Akbar was such a breath of fresh air for Surdas that, through it all, he found himself somehow breathless.

When they got to the front door of our home, Surdas asked him, "Would you like to come in?"

"I think I'd better get home. Like I said, I'm staying with my grandmother, and she would be waiting for me," Shalom Akbar responded.

Disappointed, Surdas reached out to shake his new friend's hand, when, much to his surprise, Shalom Akbar pulled Surdas into a gentle hug.

"Friends?" Shalom Akbar asked, as Surdas almost swooned in his arms.

"Friends!" Surdas exclaimed, wondering how long he could make the moment last.

The moment didn't last long, but it became more momentous as the front door swung open as the embrace was breaking, and Mother came to the rescue with an exuberant, "*There* you are! How wonderful! I was getting a little worried about Surdas, and here he's obviously been in good hands all along."

"Mother, this is Shalom Akbar," Surdas said, somewhat embarrassed. "He's a new friend who walked me home from school. I'm sorry I'm late. I should have called."

"That's OK, Baby. I'm sure there was a lot on your mind. But please remember to do it next time," he said, in his concerned Mother hen voice. "I worry when you're late, and I made some cookies in anticipation of your arrival. Why don't you and Shalom come in and have some?"

"Actually, his first name is the full Shalom Akbar, and he was just telling me that he needs to get home to his grandmother."

"Well, Mr. Impressive First Name, why don't you call your granny and tell her, that you are having milk and cookies with Surdas and his granny, and, that you'll be home shortly? My cookies are not to be missed, and neither is your story, I'm sure."

To Surdas's surprise and absolute joy, Shalom Akbar agreed. They spent the next hour or so munching on cookies and listening to his stories of traveling the world with his parents in search of some ultimate truth or spiritual satisfaction that always seemed just beyond their grasp.

"Well, I'm no expert," Mother said, as Shalom Akbar finished his story, "but maybe the truth you all were seeking wasn't out there. Maybe it's already in you, and you just need to discover, or rediscover, it.

"Like I said. I'm no expert. But I believe that truth always begins in the heart and eventually finds its way to the brain. If the heart does not understand and practice what is true, what value is there in the brain learning it?

"Do you listen to your heart," he asked gently, "or have you only heard the hearts and minds of others? You've told us what others want and expect of you. But what do *you* want and expect of you?"

As Shalom Akbar was working out an answer to the question, Mother interrupted by saying, "You don't have to answer right now, Sweetie. I didn't mean to put you on the spot. And, I know your name carries a heavy burden, the whole Jewish-Arabic thing. I can see it in your face. And if you decide to carry it, that's your prerogative.

"But at least here, whenever we're together, why don't we keep things a little lighter? We can start with an abbreviated nickname like Shak. I think we all can relax into that. What do you think?"

"That's cool!" Shak replied. "I like it! I like it a lot. I've never had a nickname. What do you think, Surdas? You can call me Shak too, whenever you'd like."

"I like!" Surdas smiled. "I definitely like."

"Well, I probably should be getting back," Shak announced as he got up from the table. "Thank you—"

"Mother!" Mother interrupted. "Everyone calls me Mother and I would particularly like it if Surdas's new friend felt comfortable enough to call me that too."

"Thank you, Mother," he replied politely. "It's an honor. Thank you too, Surdas. You made my day. I'll see you tomorrow."

"Bye, Shak!" Surdas laughed, delighted by the whole course of events. "You made my day too."

"So cool!" Shak replied, as he left. "It's all so cool!"

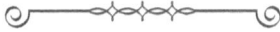

Ten

As Mother and Surdas brought the dishes and glasses into the kitchen, Mother asked if this was just a friend like Cayenne or someone with a little more potential.

"Shak isn't really gay," he replied, sounding a bit disappointed. "Then again, he isn't exactly straight either."

"Isn't that just about everyone?" Mother asked. "It's so confusing. Bisexual always meant goodbye sexual in my book. There's enough competition on either side without dragging in a couple of billion more."

"He's not bisexual either," Surdas explained. "He's taken a few vows of abstinence in some of the spiritual paths he studied, and he doesn't think in terms of sex or sexual identity."

"Even the asexual think in terms of sex and sexual identity, Sweetie. He may not want to, but I guarantee you he does."

"Huh?" Surdas questioned.

"You really like him, don't you?" Mother asked, knowingly.

"Yeah! But it's kind of frustrating. I might as well be banging my head against the wall."

"He's as young and confused as you are, Sweetie," Mother responded, thoughtfully. "Give it some time and maybe it will be his head you'll be banging against ... and I did not just say that. What I meant to say is that maybe he'll eventually figure things out and come around.

"And nobody should be banging anybody's head against the wall, except maybe me banging my own. So, perhaps I'll just quit while I'm way behind, because I'm starting to feel like one; and I'm obviously a bit rusty at this."

"You're doing perfectly fine," Surdas laughed. "And it's always important to hear things on a level that gets through to you. Shak may never come around, but I should at least give us both the opportunity for him to do so. So, thank you. I feel better already."

"That's wonderful, Sweetie," Mother said, somewhat relieved. "Just remember that often the flower that blooms from a new relationship is a friendship, not a courtship, or love affair. Cherish the flower for what it is."

"I understand, Mother. I learned enough from my relationship with Chris not to turn a friendship flower into a wedding bouquet. I couldn't see the difference then. Hopefully, I can feel the difference now."

"How did I get so lucky to wind up with a grandson like you?" Mother lovingly asked, as he drew Surdas into a warm hug.

"I guess you picked the right flower!" Surdas laughed, nuzzling into the hug.

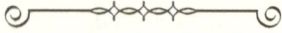

Eleven

Early that same evening Cayenne stopped by our house on his way to his lesson with the aunts. He was extremely friendly and acted as though what happened earlier in the afternoon had never happened at all. Surdas was so happy to find him in good humor, that he didn't bring it up. Nor did he mention Shak's full name, or new nickname, for fear of ruining Cayenne's mood.

"Your aunts promised me they would have a few outfits for me to try on tonight as part of my burst into stardom," Cayenne gleamed. "You have to come with me and tell me what you think. I know you can't see them, but I still want your support and vision, if you know what I mean."

"I know what you mean, but I don't know how much help I'll be," Surdas smiled, hoping to mend, or at least whitewash, whatever offense he splintered. "But I'll be more than happy to keep you company."

"Twinkle, twinkle little star," Aunt Sue exclaimed, as they arrived at the aunts' house. "And you brought our little sunshine with you. I may have to put on my sunglasses if it gets any brighter in here.

"It looks like we're going to have to conjure up more magic than we thought, Allie. It's double, double, toil and trouble."

"I'm just here for support, Auntie," Surdas explained, "not for the dress rehearsal."

"Pantyhose, girdles, and brassieres are for support, Sweetie," he laughed. "Drag is an experience, not a rehearsal, and it is time you were dressed for it."

"I don't think so," Surdas said uneasily.

"Good!" Aunt Allie exclaimed. "The first time is always easier when you don't think about it."

And before he knew what had hit him, Surdas was up on a platform dressed only in his briefs with all this silky material being wrapped around him.

"Cayenne! Are you going through this too?" he called out uncomfortably.

"YES!" Cayenne screamed in sheer joy. "Isn't it FABULOUS? I'm about to have an orgasm."

"Don't do it on the aunts' material or it will be your last one," Surdas chuckled, still uncomfortable. "I'm glad that at least *you're* excited."

"Who are you kidding, Mr. I'm-Here-For-Support," Cayenne laughed. "You have some bolly wood going on over there. I don't think you'll need any additional support in the arousal area."

"Ooh! You're right, Honey," Aunt Sue chimed in.

"That's practically open carry. We're going to have to get a holster for that bad boy."

"Oh! Like all this isn't embarrassing enough …" Surdas started to say as his thought process was suddenly interrupted by Aunt Allie slipping God-knows-what up his legs to tuck in the only part of him that apparently had a mind of its own.

"There! Uniquely eunuch," Aunt Sue laughed, as he smoothed out the area where the offending bulge had been. "Now let's move on to appropriate projectiles for the bosom area."

"This may be getting a little out of hand, Auntie," Surdas objected. "I think I have enough projectiles."

"Nonsense!" Aunt Sue chuckled. "You'll love it! Everyone knows that once you go rack you never go back."

And just when you started to think that there is no such thing as the cavalry arriving on time—the bugle blew. Once again, Mother came to the rescue.

"Exactly what do you think you two dragged-out old queens are doing to my grandson?" he howled at the aunts, who must have looked like deer in headlights during hunting season.

"It's OK, Mother," Surdas said, taking over the role of cavalry. "The aunts were just showing Cayenne some pointers and I volunteered to help as a model. Aunt Allie was just helping me out of whatever this is that I'm wearing."

"Well, I would hope so," Mother said, calming down. "You look much cuter as a boy, and you certainly didn't appear very comfortable in that outfit. Let's change you back into Surdas, and then I'll help show little Cayenne here how to really do drag."

"Yea! The team is back!" Aunt Sue exclaimed. "Let's take it up a notch from a practice runway walk and move straight up to a real drag race. Let's show little Pepper here how celestial bodies can easily outshine the stars they're impersonating."

"Can I go first?" Aunt Allie asked, sincerely.

"Of course, Dear," Aunt Sue snickered. "You've always kind of been the costar in a one-man show anyway. You go first, and that way he'll know the difference between star-dumb and stardom."

"You'd be the former if you thought I didn't catch that," Aunt Allie said with a chuckle. "Your sour grapes have been around so long they've turned to sour raisins. Even your issues have issues. I'll teach Cayenne how to make the audience laugh with you, and you can teach him how to make them laugh at you."

"Well! Get you, Allie Blabber and the forty peeves," Aunt Sue huffed, obviously caught off guard by Aunt Allie's clever retort.

"That's Lesson Number One, Cayenne," Aunt Allie laughed. "Never let someone else's light turn you into a shadow."

"Got it!" Cayenne laughed. "What's Lesson Number Two?"

"Nothing is the only thing that ever gets accomplished

by doing nothing," Aunt Allie said confidently. "Let's get to work."

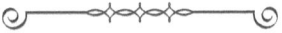

Twelve

Surdas was not really sure how many clouds there are above Cloud Nine, but Cayenne was certainly there when he met him before school the next day. He effused endlessly about the wigs, the costumes, the makeup, the lip-syncing, and the dance moves.

"I'm going to learn to do most of the impersonating my-self," he said confidently. "No lip-syncing! I'm pretty sure that I can sound like almost any famous female performer and, like Mother and your aunts, I can always compensate for any missed high notes with a little bit of humor.

"I was born to do this, Surdas. If RuPaul and Madonna had a like-a-virgin love child, I'd be it. I'm going to be so hot, I'll have to change my name to Pepper Spray because my audience's eyes will be left inflamed. I'll be over-the-top from top to bottom. Look at me. Think about it. It has to be destiny."

"You know what they say," Surdas added, with a grin. "It's not the destiny. It's the journey."

"I like that," Cayenne said, with a smile in his voice. "I think there's more Mother in you than anyone realized."

"It gets to be a family trait," Surdas laughed. "If you don't become clever, you're not paying attention."

Surdas couldn't believe how positive and happy Cayenne sounded during their conversation. So, he was more than surprised when Cayenne's voice quickly changed, and his mood suddenly became dark again.

"What's wrong?" Surdas asked, unaware of Shak's approach. "You sound upset again."

"Seasons change, and so do I," Cayenne said coldly. "And you obviously need not wonder why, since it looks like it's time for Pepper to get the brush-off, and the new exotic spice to flavor the day."

"Shak's coming?" Surdas volunteered too excitedly.

"Who the hell is Shak?" Cayenne grumbled, quite angrily. "And just how many new boyfriends do you have now anyway?"

"No new boyfriends," Surdas said, defensively. "I don't have any boyfriends at all. Shak is Shalom Akbar. It's the new nickname that Mother gave him. Cool! Right?"

And before Surdas could say another word, Cayenne was off with a departing, "Not cool ... more like frigid! I imagine you think the whole world needs one of your cute little nicknames."

"Pepper wait!" Surdas called, trying to be cute and defuse the situation.

"Your 'Pepper' is salt in the wounds," he said, as his

voice trailed away. "Have fun shacking up with your new friend Shak."

"Did I scare your friend away again?" Shak asked seriously, when he arrived a few seconds later.

"I don't know what his problem is," Surdas said honestly. "It's like he's bipolar all of a sudden. One minute he's friendly and the next he's off in a huff. It's as though he's finding problems where none exist."

"Maybe he likes you more than you realize and is jealous of any new friendships," Shak responded. "Maybe he thinks I'm some sort of threat."

"Cayenne and I are just friends," Surdas said sincerely, probably trying to stress the point more than he had to. "He even jokes that we're sisters. I'm pretty sure the only thing he's serious about is being a drag star and learning from Mother and Aunts Sue and Allie how to dress and perform on stage."

"Maybe," Shak replied, "but as a friend, I think you should sit him down and talk to him honestly. Whatever the problem is, if you're not a part of it, maybe you can at least be a part of the solution. Either way, as a friend, you should at least try."

"Sometimes you sound just like Mother," Surdas said, with a smile.

"I'm taking that as a compliment," he laughed, "Now come on, we're both going to be late for class. Let me walk you to yours."

"I've always depended on the kindness of strangers," Surdas responded, joining in on the laugh.

Normal Vision?

"If I didn't know better, I'd admit that you'd find few as strange as me" Shak said confidently. "But I think I'm beginning to know better."

Thirteen

After his first class that day, Surdas asked Cayenne if he would walk him home after school and stop for coffee at the local shop along the way. He was surprised when Cayenne said yes immediately, without any objection or asking any questions. While he wasn't overly friendly, he at least seemed a bit calmer.

Later, when Surdas met up with Shak, he told him that he was taking his advice about talking to Cayenne. He said Cayenne would walk him home after school. Shak thought it was a great idea, but he took Surdas's cell phone and put his number on the speed dial, just in case he had to fill in for the rest of the trip home. He became Surdas's thirteenth speed dial number. Suddenly, Surdas was in love with that lucky number.

Cayenne was late in meeting him after school, but Surdas was sure he would show. He reasoned that Cayenne is not the type to let you down, even if he's upset with you. Cayenne didn't offer any excuse for being late when he finally arrived, and Surdas wasn't about to ask. He was just happy that Cayenne was there.

Oddly, they walked and talked all the way to the café as though there had never been anything wrong. Cayenne seemed so at ease as they ordered a couple of frozen lattes and sat down to enjoy them, that Surdas felt confident enough to jump right in and ask him what was bothering him.

"You really *are* blind," Cayenne said, in a tone that had Surdas imagine he was shaking his head in disbelief. "And when it comes to me, I guess you're deaf and dumb too. And I don't mean dumb in terms of speaking."

Surdas was stunned. But he immediately knew what Cayenne was referring to, and that he was right. And he knew Shak was also right when he told him that there might be more to Cayenne's feelings for him than he had allowed himself to imagine. But what to say next? This was not a time for jokes or clever retorts.

"I'm sorry!" Surdas blurted out. "I guess you're right. I just thought we were really good friends. I love our friendship, and I love you as a friend. I just never thought of anything deeper or stronger."

"Until now," Cayenne interrupted, obviously hurt.

"If you're talking about Shak, we're just really good friends too," Surdas responded.

"Only deeper and stronger," he interrupted again, "especially on your part."

"It's just different," Surdas tried to explain.

"Exactly!" Cayenne said, sounding even more upset. "And that's where you're deaf, dumb, and blind."

"No! You don't understand," Surdas tried again to explain. "Shak's taken all these vows of chastity and stuff. We don't have anything more than a friendship."

"Listen to your words and be honest with yourself," Cayenne said. "The only reason you don't have a different relationship is because he doesn't want it. Imagine if he just didn't want it with you. Imagine if you could see how much he wanted it with someone else. Imagine how you would feel. And then imagine what it's like for me.

"I tried to be everything I could for you, and you never really saw me. You never really heard me. All you saw and heard was what you wanted to see and hear. And if my references to sight offend you, you better suck it up, because your blindness toward me offends me."

As hurt as Surdas felt by his attack, he also felt that Cayenne was right, and his response justifiable. He was trying to formulate an apologetic response, yet, all the while Cayenne was speaking, Surdas could also hear someone in the background saying things like, "Holy shit! Puppy faggots!" and "It's a couple of pansy puffers!"

The offending voice probably said a few other things, but Surdas was trying so hard to concentrate on what Cayenne was saying, and trying to formulate a response, that his mind couldn't help ignoring the rest of it. But apparently Cayenne's wasn't.

"Blow it out your ass you fat bigoted moron," Cayenne yelled, turning his attention away from Surdas and to the offending voice. "There's enough shit going on here without you spewing more out of that hideous mouth of yours. So, why don't you mind your own business, and just go slither away and find whatever rock you crawled out from underneath? The world is ugly enough without you adding to it. And it would be hard-pressed to find someone as ugly as you."

And then turning his attention back to Surdas, he said, "Wait here. This whole thing is suffocating. I need to catch my breath and get some fresh air. Everything is too stifling in here!" And with that, he suddenly got up and left.

Surdas pleaded with him to come back, but there was no response. He waited a while, hoping that Cayenne would return. But after more than a few minutes, he became worried, because he knew that Cayenne wouldn't leave him alone in the café, no matter how angry he was with him.

He asked their waitress if she knew where his friend went, and she said he went out the back way followed by the older guy he was arguing with.

Surdas panicked. Suddenly the offending voice thundered in his head. He knew Cayenne must be in trouble. He asked the waitress to direct him to the back door. It wasn't until later that he found out what happened in the meantime.

Apparently, Cayenne was cooling off in the alley behind the café when the stranger, who was insulting them, suddenly appeared.

"That was quite a hissy fit you pulled inside, Girly

Boy," the stranger sneered. "Maybe you need a real man to straighten you out."

"If I see one, I'll let you know," Cayenne replied, a bit shaken. "Now if you'll excuse me, my friend is waiting for me inside where there are probably some real men."

Cayenne tried to leave, but the stranger blocked his path.

"I'll show you what a real man can do," the man replied sarcastically. "Your friend is blind, right? And you left him in the dark. You're such a good friend. I'm sure that he's used to it, so he can stay there a bit longer.

"So, tell me, what are you anyway … like half girl, half faggot?"

"If you had half a brain," Cayenne said, "you wouldn't be asking. But since you did, if you have to wrap your head around something, try making it a telephone pole."

"You're a feisty little bitch, aren't you?" the guy replied.

"And you're an idiot—and I'm out of here. That's what I am," Cayenne responded anxiously, as he tried to rush past the stranger.

"Whoa! Whoa! Whoa!" the guy laughed sinisterly, as he grabbed Cayenne by the arm and blocked his exit. "I'm pretty sure that both the girly half and the faggot half want to give me a blowjob to apologize for being so rude."

"I think all of me wants you to blow off, jerk," Cayenne responded angrily. "That's your blowjob. You're obviously a jerk of all trades, masturbator of none. Now let me go."

"Don't play with me, faggot," the man said, as he threw Cayenne to the ground. "I'll send you straight to hell if you play with me. This is what people like you do; and this is what you're going to do."

"Screw you!" Cayenne screamed, as he tried to get up. "I wouldn't do or play with you even if you had something to play with. "So do this," he said, as he gave the guy the middle finger.

"You're the one who's going to get fucked, Girly Boy," the guy growled, as he punched Cayenne in the midsection, doubling him over and sending him back to the ground. "Don't make me do that to your face. I don't want to get blood all over my prick when you give me that apology."

"Probably wouldn't take much blood," Cayenne jeered, with absolute disdain, "maybe a drop or two at most. It's got to be just as small as your brain. I'd draw you a picture, but I'd probably have to use stick figures for you to understand."

With that, the stranger picked Cayenne up and flung him into a row of garbage cans saying, "Have it your way, Girly Boy."

It was at the sound of that crash that Surdas walked through the back door and into the alley.

"Cayenne are you here?" he called anxiously. "Are you all right? I heard a crash. What's going on?"

"Go back inside, Surdas, please," Cayenne pleaded, obviously in pain. "I'll be back in a minute."

Surdas could hear that he was not only in pain but scared, and he wasn't about to leave him alone.

"Just tell me what's going on, Cayenne," Surdas demanded. "Are you hurt? Do you need help? Is that guy bothering you?"

Before he could respond, the strange voice said, "Perhaps the blind faggot would like to go first. Your little girly friend here was about to give me a blowjob. Do you want to go first? Or are you more the back door type?"

"Don't listen to him, Surdas. He's a complete moron. Run back inside please," Cayenne cried. "Go back inside before he hurts you too."

"There is no way I'm leaving you, Cayenne," Surdas swore. "The only one who better leave is this jerk."

"So, it looks like the little brown one wants to stay and go first," the venomous voice called out, and suddenly Surdas could feel the hostility approaching.

"Please go back inside, Surdas, before the fucker gets to you. Please!" Cayenne pleaded.

"Think, Cayenne, think," Surdas shouted. "Remember the clock."

"What?" he answered, perplexed. "What are you talking about?"

"Remember the clock?" the threatening voice mocked, as it drew closer. "What is this … some sort of stall, or perhaps a game of blind man's bluff?"

"Cayenne Think! Remember the soccer story about Chris and the clock," Surdas pleaded.

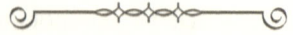

Fourteen

One of Cayenne's favorite stories about Surdas's childhood was about the time that his cousin Chris taught him how to play the goalie position in soccer … not an easy task for a blind eleven-year-old.

Chris knew all too well that he was Surdas's hero. It was not a responsibility he took lightly. One day when Surdas was reveling in the excitement of yet another of his best friend's shutout wins, he gushed about how proud he was of him, and how he wished he could truly understand what it was like to be a goalie like Chris.

"Well then, let's do it!" Chris exclaimed excitedly, without hesitation. "Let's make you a goalie."

"Yeah right!" Surdas laughed. "All I would need is for the opposing players to keep aiming at my head. Then at least I could stop some of the shots that the players with really good aim take. Or did you forget, that for me, all the shots would be shots in the dark?"

"The eyes don't always have it," Chris assured him,

with what must have been a gleam in his. "And your eyes are just a small part of you. Everything else about you is exceptional, so we'll work with the exceptional parts."

"What do you mean?" Surdas asked excitedly.

"I'm going to teach you a few martial arts moves, and then you're going to become a clock."

"A clock? I think you have been stopping too many of those soccer balls with your head," Surdas laughed. "Even if any of that made sense, what would being a clock have to do with being a goalie?"

"Patience, grasshopper! Patience," Chris chuckled. "It takes time to be a clock. Let's begin with the hands of the clock."

Every day for weeks, Chris taught Surdas how to use his hands and legs as though he was fending off an attack. After each lesson, he would have Surdas assume a time position of an imaginary clock using his arms or legs. When he got the movements and time positions down, Chris would toss a soccer ball and call out a time marking the position of the incoming ball. The ball would be incoming at the minute hand position with the hour hand indicating the angle of trajectory.

Surdas felt like it took him forever to get it all down, but Chris never lost patience and encouraged him every step of the way. Eventually, it all sank in. Chris was able to kick or throw the ball with greater and greater speed and, for the most part, Surdas was able to stop, or at least deflect, most of them. So now, he not only had a chance of kicking or swatting away a ball in a smaller practice goal, but he could also, to some extent, even defend himself against an attack.

Using the smaller practice goal so he wouldn't have to dive at shots, Chris had his soccer teammates challenge Surdas in goal. With Chris standing behind the goal chiming out times, Surdas managed to stop all but a dozen, or so, of the fifty shots fired his way. Everyone was so impressed that they carried him off the field. Best of all, it turned out to be the worst performance of the many practices that followed.

Surdas will forever smile whenever he thinks of those games. He will forever cherish the time, the minutes and hours that turned into days and weeks, that Chris spent teaching him. Chris is forever his teacher. Surdas is forever a goalie. Thanks to his beloved timekeeper, Surdas is forever a clock.

Fifteen

"The clock Cayenne! Remember the clock!" Surdas yelled. "Think ... the clock!"

"What clock?" a still confused Cayenne cried. "I don't understand! Just run!"

"Remember the soccer story ... Chris ... the goalie ... the clock!" Surdas yelled louder, sensing the menacing presence almost upon him.

"Oh! Shit! Eight-forty-five!" Cayenne screamed, with little time to be sure of himself.

His eight-forty-five estimate may not have been perfect timing, but it was close enough for Surdas to swat the stranger's hand away and grab enough of his shirt to soundly swing him off-balance in the direction of Cayenne's voice.

As the attacker tumbled to the ground, Surdas heard the guy crash into the remaining garbage cans. While the stunned stranger lay there, Surdas could hear Cayenne kicking and throwing whatever trash cans and lids he could find on top of the guy. The noise and Cayenne's expletives made such a racket, that most of the café staff, some of the guests, and eventually the police showed up.

Through all the chaos, no matter how much he protested, no one bought the stranger's story that the frail kid and his blind friend propositioned him, and then attacked him when he refused. However, they did believe, without question, Surdas's story of how the stranger knocked him to the ground; and how his brave friend fiercely fought off a sexual attack from the much larger and stronger man, who witnesses testified insulted and threatened them in the café.

The man was arrested, the café staff helped clean up Surdas and Cayenne, and John was called to pick them up. While they waited for an extremely anxious John to arrive, Cayenne asked Surdas, "Why did you change the story?"

Surdas told him, "It would be better for my family politically, and for you socially, if most of the publicity surrounded you. After all, who could resist an irresistibly beautiful Amazon who just fended off some barbarian?"

"I'm sorry about the whole jealous thing," Cayenne said sheepishly, as they waited. "You're a really good friend … my best friend. I think I was afraid of losing you to someone else. Can you forgive me?"

"Don't be sorry, because there is nothing to forgive," Surdas said sincerely. "I've certainly been there. I'm an expert on jealousy. And I unfortunately have a history of being blind in more ways than just my vision, as both you and Chris can attest to. I wasn't always that way. I used to be very intuitive and focused on the needs of others. But I think that I became so used to being fussed over, and the center of attention, that I allowed myself to become self-centered. So, I'm the one who should apologize."

"I guess that I'm at the opposite end of the same spectrum," Cayenne admitted. "I'm so used to not being fussed over and not being the center of anyone's attention, that I became self-centered too. I wanted you to be someone you're not, so I could be something I'm not."

"The important thing is that we're centered now," Surdas added. "One of the many things Chris taught me was that real friends understand when things like this happen. And when they understand, there is no need for forgiveness, just understanding, just healing. Now we understand each other. We're real friends. I imagine that we'll always be real friends.

"Mother always says, 'Live in the now and you'll give yourself the best present you possibly can.' The double entendre has not been lost on me. We're back to being best friends now. What better present is there than that?"

"I'm also sorry about the way I acted toward Shalom Akbar," Cayenne added, making Surdas smile at the first time he said his name correctly. "I don't even know him, and I never gave him a chance for us to know each other. So, I also want to apologize to him … in person, of course. I hope he is as understanding as you are."

"I'm sure you'll find that he understands far more than I did," Surdas said, with a smile. "He's not nearly as blind as I am."

"But there's still one remaining problem that troubles me," Cayenne added.

"What's that?" Surdas asked, a little worried.

"If you guys are going to be spending a lot of time together," he laughed, "your Shak is going to have to find someone who I can double date with. I haven't had much luck in that department, and I'm certainly not going to trust your vision."

"Funny!" Surdas said "But Shak and I aren't dating. We really are just friends."

"I'm the one who isn't blind, remember!" Cayenne said, a little more seriously. "That look on your face is the same as the look on his when you're together. I know. I've secretly been keeping an eye on you both. The mystery of the clock may be that it takes time, but you can still read its face. Just keep yourself in the proper position, and when he finally takes his shot, the ball, or in this case the plural, will be in your hands."

"Funny," Surdas laughed, "but I'm still pretty sure that I'm the only one playing."

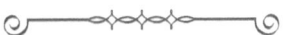

Sixteen

News travels fast in small towns. And, although Surdas wasn't sure how he heard it, as soon as Shak did, he came running over to our home to make sure that Surdas was OK.

"You must be Surdas's new friend, Shak," John said, as he answered the door. "We've already heard a lot about you, so it's a pleasure to finally meet you."

"I'll take it from here, Bapu," Surdas said, rushing somewhat embarrassed toward the door.

"Nonsense! Bapu Gene and I would love to meet your new friend," John laughed, with some sort of parental tone that sounded sure to add to Surdas's embarrassment. "Gene should be right down. Come on in Shak and sit for a while. Let's get to know each other a little better."

"I didn't mean to intrude," Shak apologized. "I heard about what happened at the café, and I just wanted to make sure that everything was OK with Surdas. I probably should have just called."

Surdas could tell by the tone of Shak's voice that he undoubtedly sensed Surdas's unease at the heard-a-lot-about-you comment and John's let's-find-out-more-about-this-guy parental tone, and was trying to avoid any further embarrassment on Surdas's part, and on his own.

"Nonsense," John's voice rang. "We're all glad you're here. Why not come in and sit for a while, and we can all get acquainted? It's always a pleasure to finally meet someone you've heard so much about."

"I think the boys probably need to talk about this on their own in Surdas's room," I said softly, as I came to our son's rescue from what must have seemed like out of nowhere, and ushered the boys up the stairs. "We'll have plenty of opportunity to visit with Shak another time, I'm sure."

"I just wanted to make Surdas's new friend feel more at ease and at home," John said defensively.

"And I think I just did," I laughed, as I closed Surdas's bedroom door behind them and whispered, "You owe me one, Buddy."

"Are you OK?" Shak asked, as he hugged Surdas as soon as the door closed. "I was so worried about you."

"I'm fine," Surdas assured him, "just a little bruised. That's two bullies within a very short period of time. Did someone pin some sort of gay bullseye on my back?"

"I wish I could've been there to help you," Shak said sincerely. "I somehow knew I should've been there. I wish I had listened to myself."

"I don't think that would've been a good idea," Surdas laughed. "The guy suffered enough without having to grapple with your temper. And in the end, you would've been the one suffering the most from the guilt of giving in to it."

"You know me well, grasshopper," Shak responded, with a smile in his voice. "So, tell me from the beginning what happened."

Over the next fifteen or twenty minutes, Surdas told Shak the story as honestly as he remembered it. It all happened so quickly, he wasn't sure if he remembered everything.

Shak asked Surdas, "Were you really scared?"

Surdas joked, "It was akin to reading a sign in braille that says, 'Danger! Do Not Touch!'"

The comment broke the somber mood and made Shak laugh.

Shak said, "I understand the reasons you changed the story of what actually happened, but it makes me sad that people won't ever know what a real hero you are.

"I'm sorry that Cayenne was hurt by our friendship. Does he understand now that there really isn't any reason to be jealous?" he asked, as the daggered question pierced deeper into Surdas's very being.

"I'm sure he does," Surdas said, as cheerfully as he could. "I think that maybe we can all be friends now."

"Good! I'd really like that," Shak said, all too cheerfully. "You two look so cool together. I would never want to come between you."

Stab me one more time, my friend, Surdas thought, trying not to take the last comment suggestively, *and one of us is going to die.*

Shak must have mistaken the look on Surdas's face for something else because he said, "You still appear a bit shaken and upset by everything that happened today. You should rest. Suppose we lay down on the bed, and I'll hold you for a while. Maybe it will help you feel better, and you'll be able to fall asleep."

Surdas thought that almost sounded schizophrenic after all Shak said prior. But it was also everything he wanted to hear. So, he did as Shak suggested, and, after a little while, he comfortably fell asleep in Shak's arms.

Surdas must have needed the rest more than he realized because he fell into a deep sleep. When he awoke the next morning, Shak was gone, and all that was left was the phantom feel of Shak's arms around him.

Later that morning, Surdas told Cayenne all about his conversation with Shak the night before, and how Shak held him until he fell asleep.

"See, I told you. 'Methinks he doth protest too much,'" Cayenne declared. "It sounds rather romantic if you ask me."

"I wish that were the case," Surdas sighed, "but I think he's so caught up in the destiny of his name that he doesn't allow himself to see anything else before him."

"I think that it's the whole can't see the forest for the trees thing," Cayenne insisted. "He needs you to help him see what he can't see on his own."

"You're asking someone who's blind to help someone

with vision to see," Surdas said, trying to use humor to change the subject.

"I'm asking someone with vision to open up their mind, to help someone else open theirs," Cayenne replied. "Take him to someplace special, someplace you're sure he'll love, someplace where it's just the two of you, and see if his destiny doesn't start to unravel a bit."

"I don't know," Surdas said, somewhat afraid of what he might find out.

"Exactly!" Cayenne said confidently. "You don't know. And it's time you did."

That afternoon Shak joined Cayenne and Surdas for lunch in the school cafeteria. Not only didn't anyone bother them, but they suddenly seemed to be the center of attention, as the school was abuzz about how Cayenne had overpowered the stranger who attacked the two boys. Even though he never mentioned it, Surdas could tell Cayenne was enjoying the notoriety. He never seemed so cheerful.

"You sure seem to be very popular today," Shak finally remarked, not revealing that he knew the real story. "I have a feeling that a lot of people want to hear the hero's journey."

"We'll see how it translates over the next couple of days," Cayenne chuckled. "When you go from a comical character to a comic book hero, it's easy to slip back to the comical character when your exploits are over. For now, I'm just basking in the peaceful lack of insults and sneers."

"Who knows, it might even lead to something romantic," Surdas laughed. "The possibilities are endless."

"Maybe!" Cayenne chuckled again. "But, changing the subject, weren't you talking about showing Shak that place that means a lot to you after school? It sounds really cool. And, if he walks you home, it will free me up to explore some of the possibilities you mentioned."

There was this awkward silence as Surdas wasn't sure how to respond or even where to go if Shak said yes. About a minute into his embarrassment, Shak broke the silence by asking, "Cat got your tongue? Where are we going?"

"It's a secret," Surdas said, trying to stall.

"A favorite place and a secret?" Shak asked, sounding somewhat excited. "I think we both have something to look forward to."

"Of course," Surdas responded, as the cliff by the lake that he and Chris often visited came to mind. "Even though I can't see it, I think it's beautiful. And I think you will too."

"It's a date," Shak replied, probably not realizing that, at least for Surdas, it was just that.

Seventeen

When they arrived at the lake and Shak saw the waterfall and overhang on the cliff where Chris and Surdas would often sit, he remarked that he could see why this place was so special to Surdas. It was positively beautiful. He laughed when Surdas told him about the first time Chris took him there, convinced him to climb the cliff, and then had to save him when they fell into the lake. He laughed even harder when Surdas told him it happened a second time shortly thereafter and he had to be saved all over again.

"Do you want to try for three?" Shak asked cheerfully.

"What?" Surdas laughed. "Do you want to throw me in the lake so you can save me too?"

"No, silly! Do you want to try to climb the cliff with me this time? I'm a good rock climber, and I can stand right behind you the way Chris did, and guide you all the way up."

Surdas was about to remind him what happened the

last time with Chris standing right behind him, when he suddenly remembered that he wanted to do anything he could with Shak, even if it meant falling into the lake again. And he certainly wasn't about to tell him, if it happened again, he now knew how to swim.

"OK! If you're sure," he responded, as meekly as possible, "but make sure you hold me tight."

So, they took off their sandals, rolled up their pant legs, and started climbing, with Shak pressed firmly against Surdas. Halfway up, around the same spot where Chris and Surdas fell, Surdas shuttered, not because he was falling or afraid, but because he was sure that he felt Shak's excitement pressing against him. Shak felt the shutter and pressed against him even more to reassure him. Now Surdas was reassured, not only of the safety … but also of the excitement.

Surdas didn't know if Shak's excitement would ever lead to anything, but at least he knew that Mother was right that everyone is sexual in one way or another. And Cayenne was right that Shak liked him.

When they reached the overhang and sat down, Shak wiped the dirt and pebbles off Surdas's feet even before Surdas had a chance to do so. Surdas was so impressed with his kindness and thoughtfulness, and the gentleness of his touch, that he wanted to kiss him. But of course, discretion being the better part of valor, he chickened out and thought better of it. He remembered that if you count your chickens before they hatch, you may wind up with egg on your face.

As they sat there, Shak said, "You know, I try every day to see all the beauty that surrounds me as though it were my last day, and it would be the last time I'd see it. It helps keep me focused in the present, and it helps me to appreciate how divinity is always without and within me. And yet, I must admit, that this is the most beautiful, the most divine moment I've ever experienced. And I'm sure it's because I'm seeing it with and through you. Thank you! I truly see all that you see in it."

And, as though his words had come quickly back to haunt him, he humbly apologized for using so many sight references.

"There's no need to apologize," Surdas assured him. "You probably won't believe this, but once when I had an accident and was unconscious, and they thought that I might die, Lord Krishna showed me many different creatures, objects, and colors, and allowed me to maintain the image of them when I returned. I don't know if I see them the same way as everyone else, but I have vivid memories of them all. So, when you mention something like an animal, or an object, in my mind it has an image even if it's different from yours."

"I not only believe you," Shak said confidently, "but I'll bet you see things perfectly, because Lord Krishna would not have shown them to you any other way. So now you can put the names of the colors to the images you've seen."

"What do you mean?" Surdas asked.

"Do you remember the sky?"

"Of course," Surdas responded. "I'll never forget it."

"Well, that color is blue," Shak said excitedly. "So, when anyone says blue, they are referring to some shade of color like that sky, like Lord Krishna, himself. Is he the same color as the sky?"

"Kind of, but brighter," Surdas responded.

"That's a shade," he said gleefully. "Colors come in many shades, some brighter, some deeper, some paler, even to the point where you can barely make them out. Some colors even come with a mixture of other colors. Now look at the ground that you saw. Was there grass?"

"Yes!"

"Well, grass is green, so when anyone says the color green, they're referring to some shade of the color you saw."

They continued with the colors of the Sun, the flowers and plants, the animals and birds, the sand, and the water until Surdas's mind was a giant box of crayons, or at least what he thought a giant box of crayons must look like.

They were both so ecstatic at the game-changing game, that neither one of them could speak for quite a while after it was over. Shak had colored Surdas's vision with a whole new hue. Chris had taught him how colors feel, now Shak taught him what they looked like.

Finally, Surdas smiled, and broke the silence by saying, "You and Chris have described my favorite place so brilliantly, that I am sure it is the most beautiful site I have never seen.

"Mother told me that some people say, 'beauty is in the eye of the beholder.' But he believes that it is actually in the heart of the beholder, because if it isn't there first, the eye will never see it. I know that he is right because of the visions you and Chris have given me. Their beauty is forever in my heart. That's where I behold them."

"I also know that Mother is right," Shak said, as he put his arm around Surdas's shoulder, "because the heart is where I first saw you."

"You not only took my words away before I had a chance to speak them," Surdas smiled, "but you also took my breath away."

After that, they just sat there for some time, taking in the moment and smiling at one another. Eventually, Surdas told Shak that he makes him very happy. Shak responded the way Chris once had by putting Surdas's hand to his face, allowing Surdas to feel his smile. Surdas didn't tell him that Chris had done the same. He let Shak think it was something that only they shared ... because somehow it felt that way.

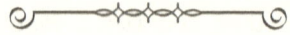

Eighteen

That evening, when Shak walked Surdas home, it became more than evident that Cayenne had something up his sleeve when he met them just outside Mother and Dad's home, and insisted that Shak join everyone for dinner. Surdas could only assume that Cayenne was not usually insistent on people staying for dinner in other people's homes and that there must have been somewhat of a conspiracy at hand with other family members.

"Hi! I'm Surdas's great-uncle, Josh," a voice said, startling the boys from behind before Shak could respond to the offer. "I understand you'll be joining us for dinner. Benji, I mean Mother, will be so excited. He lives for these things."

"It's a pleasure to meet you, sir," Shak responded. "My name is—"

"Shalom Akbar!" Uncle Josh interrupted. "I've heard much about you. You have a very impressive and beautiful name … too beautiful and important to be shortened, except among friends of course."

"I suppose that's true," Shak said sheepishly, "but it does get a little heavy at times."

"I would imagine that's true," Uncle Josh admitted. "It's an elegant blend of two cultures that often don't blend well together. But don't get me wrong, I understand the importance of nicknames, especially when you are young.

"I still call Mother, Benji, because his given name is Benjamin. His husband Tom, who everyone refers to as Dad, calls him Ben. And everyone else calls him Mother, because of his kind and gentle nature. So, nicknames are not only common, but they can also be important to the people who use them. And the nickname Shak is impressive enough in itself. I was merely reminding you not to forget the beauty you were born into. And I would stress that the name is only as heavy as the weight you put on it."

"I'll try to remember that, Sir," Shak responded, not quite knowing how else to respond. "Thank you."

"So, what do you say we get down to important issues and join the others for dinner,' Uncle Josh laughed.

"Hello! Isn't that what I said from the beginning?" Cayenne giggled. "If that introduction got any longer, we'd be eating breakfast instead of dinner."

"There's a little more of Sue in you than meets the eye," Uncle Josh chuckled. "Maybe your pseudonym should be Sue Perlative."

"Oh! This is only the beginning," Cayenne laughed. "By the time I'm finished, they'll be calling me Sue Pernova!"

"Lofty ambitions," Uncle Josh joked, as they joined the others for dinner. "It's a great attribute for a star. I'd say, for you, the sky's the limit. But I'm pretty sure even the sky couldn't contain you."

"I'm sure what he said is a compliment," Cayenne whispered to Surdas and Shak. "I just wish he'd use phrases that I didn't have to look up all the time. By the time you finally realize what he's saying, it's too late to say thank you."

The dinner gathering was rather small for one of Mother's special meals. Robbie's family was still in Albany, except for Chris who was away at college, as was Molly. Dale and Lauren were still on their honeymoon in Provincetown. Uncle Mohammed was out of the country on some important Sufi excursion. And Chip came stag because Randy was in New York City on business. That left only Mother and Dad, John and me, Aunts Sue and Allie, and of course, Uncle Josh and Chip, joining Surdas and his two friends.

Mother wasn't used to cooking for such a small crowd … so he didn't. There were three buffet tables with enough food to feed a small army. Most of it was either kosher, halal, or vegetarian since Mother had no idea what would be appropriate for someone named Shalom Akbar, who had practiced almost every form of spiritual discipline at one time or another.

As we all sat down to eat, Uncle Josh said a beautiful nondenominational prayer of thanksgiving. As he completed his prayer, Surdas surprised his friends by singing a beautiful Hindi prayer. Once again, tears filled everyone's eyes, though only he and Shak understood the words that he chanted.

Shak said, "You're singing one of Saint Surdas's poems devoted to Lord Krishna, aren't you?"

"Your education is broader than I realized," Uncle Josh responded.

Mother then introduced Shak to the gathering, since everyone hadn't met him yet. Everything was going rather smoothly until just before dessert, when the peaceful tide rolled out, and the Aunt Sue-Nami surged in.

"So, my little Shak-a-khan," Aunt Sue began, "we know our friend Cayenne here is a hot little pepper approaching drag stardom. How about you? Would you say that you're more metro, hetero, homo, bi, or A?"

A chorus of Sue and Aunt Sue rang out, but it was not enough to quell the tidal wave.

"I'm only asking because my great-nephew here is obviously heels-over-head for our handsome young guest, and, as far as I know, we don't have any closets on the property. So, if there are any skeletons, they might as well come out now."

"Don't even think of answering that soon-to-be eunuch, Baby," Mother chimed in. "Sue's class was dismissed a long time ago, and even her cigarettes don't have filters."

"I'm just saying if the meat is hot, and on the table, why not talk about the gravy?" Aunt Sue responded.

"Sometimes I wonder if even *you* know what you're saying," Mother frowned. "Joshie, why don't you take the boys into the living room while the rest of us clear the dishes over Sue's head?"

Uncle Josh and Dad dutifully escorted Shak and Surdas inside, while Cayenne hung out in the kitchen hoping to witness some action.

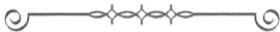

Nineteen

"So, My Boy," Uncle Josh addressed Shak, as he and Dad sat down on chairs opposite Shak and Surdas on the sofa, "I understand you have chosen a very difficult path in life."

"I suppose that's true, but I sometimes believe that it's more like it was chosen for me, Sir," Shak responded politely.

"I'm not sure I understand," Uncle Josh replied, quite perplexed. "How was it chosen for you?"

"You know," Shak shrugged, "the name, the spiritual teachings, the parental expectations … the list goes on. My parents did name me Shalom Akbar, after all … kind of heavy on the expectations, if you know what I mean."

"I see," Uncle Josh responded, with what must have been a knowing nod. "I take it then not all of the expectations are yours."

"Well, maybe not entirely," Shak said defensively. "I

mean some are, but not necessarily all of them. Mostly I just go with the flow, and try and sort things out for myself."

"I think I understand," Uncle Josh said with a smile. "I try to mind my own business when it comes to other people's affairs. The problem is that I often make their business mine. So, I hope you'll excuse me if it sounds like I'm minding yours.

"As you probably know, I like to tell stories, especially when they're true. Can I tell you one that you might find relevant, or at least interesting?"

"Of course," Shak replied, returning the smile. "Surdas told me about your wonderful stories. I'm thrilled that you're going to share one with me."

"A long time ago, when Benji, Sue, and Allie were young performers at the Kit Kat Club, there was an older gentleman from my father's congregation who would come regularly to their early performances. I say early performances because there were two performances a night, and he would always attend the first one. And I say older gentleman because he was much older than all of us.

"Anyway, Joel ... It's funny how that happens because his name just popped into my head ... Joel Steinberg.

"But anyway, Joel was this quiet, slightly built man that a good sneeze could blow away. For months he would show up at the performances, and then disappear as quickly as he appeared. He never said a word to anyone. He just stared at the performances as though he was mentally taking notes. Which it turns out, he was.

"One night, Benji surprised him by waiting for him

by the exit as he endeavored to slip out. After a brief introduction, Benji invited Joel backstage to meet the other performers. Joel was thrilled, but you could tell that he was anxious about the time. Still, the backstage visits became a part of his regular routine. But they always remained short, as he would look at his watch and say he had to run to take care of his elderly mother.

"Now Joel had to be at least seventy, if he was a day. So his mother had to be close to one hundred. Since inquiring minds want to know, little by little, Benji, Sue, and Allie discovered that Joel was the good son that his mother always wanted him to be. He became a respected lawyer. He never married, because his widowed mother needed his help. And he was never able to live the life that he truly wanted to live, because that would be totally unacceptable in his community, and especially to his mother. In other words, he was a walking, talking facade.

"And in case you haven't guessed by now, the life that he truly wanted to live was the life that Benji, Sue, and Allie were living. Apparently, since he was a little child, there was this whole alternative life going on inside of him, that he was never able to express while his mother was alive.

"Now, on more than one occasion, he asked if he might audition for our trio when his mother was gone. The others couldn't even imagine what an audition by this frail older gentleman would be like, but of course, being the mensches they are, they agreed. He appeared extremely happy with the idea, but then, a short time later, he suddenly disappeared.

"A few months later, our trio were appearing at a club in Provincetown, when Joel suddenly reappeared. It must have been a Sunday because I was there and wouldn't have been on the Sabbath. Sue and Allie had gone off with this unsavory gangster, who Sue was seeing at the time, to a savory seafood buffet somewhere further down the Cape. Benji stayed behind because, being the true performer that he was, he had to make sure everything would be perfect for that night's performances. He was thrilled to see Joel, but he had so much to do that he couldn't spend a whole lot of time with him. So, I assumed babysitting duties.

"As I'm sure you guessed, Joel told me that his mother had passed, and now that a suitable amount of time had also passed, he wanted to take Benji and the others up on their offer to let him audition for them. He wondered if they might even squeeze him into their act. He was hoping that they would let him tryout that evening after their show so that he could do it on a real stage. Again, it was a life-long dream, so the staging was important.

"As fate would have it, and fate always seems to have it, there was a major accident on the main road leading to Provincetown, and it would be hours before the road would be cleared. A distressing phone call revealed that Sue and Allie were on the wrong side of the accident, and they would probably miss that evening's performances.

"Benji was, of course, extremely anxious because their act was new to the club, and he wasn't sure if he had enough material to do a solo show. With a confidence as unexpected as the gesture itself, Joel volunteered to step in.

He assured Benji that he had everything he needed if Benji would just give him the opportunity to prove himself.

"Benji must have been feeling extremely desperate because he accepted the offer without any hesitation, and, even more surprisingly, without as much as a hint of an audition. He never even asked who or what Joel would be performing. He just exclaimed, 'Go for it!' and scampered off to do the hundred other things he had to do. I imagine that if someone throws you a lifeline, you really don't care what the line looks like.

"Anyway, when it came time for Joel to take the stage, he appeared in this cute little black French dress. I say black French dress because when Benji asked him how he would like to be introduced, he said, 'Edith Pilaf,' so I assume it was French.

"The club was noisy as Joel took to the stage. Benji and I both worried that no one would be able to hear such a frail little man over the sounds of laughter and conversation. By the time he sang the opening lines of *La Vie en Rose* without music accompaniment, however, you could not only hear a pin drop, but you could see every jaw in the house drop as well. If you didn't know better, you would swear that he had to be lip-syncing to an original recording. It was pure Piaf perfection. The club erupted into one of the loudest standing ovations I've ever heard in my life. It seemed like it went on forever. Then, when the audience finally quieted, he sang Piaf's *Non, je ne regrette rien* to the same type of ovation. A huge star was born right before our eyes.

"But he wasn't finished yet. He asked Benji to entertain the audience as he made a quick change, and returned as 'Maria's Callus' in this tight silk wrap that made him look like the diva herself. He began singing *Casta Diva*, Maria Callas's most famous aria from the opera *Norma*. It was hardly the type of performance that you would expect in a drag show, but it was so pure, so beautiful, so Callas, that the audience was entranced. Before they could give him the type of response they had given before, and that he surely deserved, he tore off the wrap exposing a sexy gypsy outfit, and began singing the *Habanera* aria from the opera *Carmen*. The eruption was even louder than all the others. You could hear the audience singing the chorus, the bravos, and the applause the entire length of Commercial Street. Crowds gathered outside the club to find out what all the excitement was about. The buzz was electric. The club owner was so caught up in the swell that he offered Joel a headlining position for the rest of the season.

"Our frail little lawyer was the toast of the town, and he spent the rest of the night celebrating his performance with dozens of adoring fans. I can't even begin to imagine how much it meant for the life he always wanted, for the life that was meant to be, to suddenly burst into stardom. He was in heaven.

"The next morning, when Benji went to his room to show him the amazing reviews of his performance, he had literally gone there. The excitement of finally being who and what he had always wanted to be was too much for the heart that always desired it.

"You're probably asking yourself by now why am I telling you this long-winded story about someone who so few people now remember. It's because I can't help but imagine how happy this man would have been, how fortunate everyone who would have the opportunity to see him perform would have been, had he allowed himself to live the life he always wanted for himself. He had been granted an amazing gift that he unfortunately locked away and displayed all too briefly, and all too late."

"That's an amazing story," Shak responded, with a slight smile. "And the message certainly isn't lost on me. I get the point. I really do. But, I think there's a difference because that guy knew deep down inside what he always wanted to be. I'm not sure what I want to be. I'm not sure of anything. I'm still seeking. Shouldn't I just keep going until I'm sure?"

"I'm going to answer your question with another question, because that's what rabbis do. Are you really the one doing the seeking, or are there others seeking for you? It's an important question because the gift you have been given is as great as any that Joel had. It is the gift of your life, as precious and important as any other. Only you can decide the best way to use that gift. Only you can decide who and what you truly are. If you spend your life waiting to become that person, you may never be that person. A disciple follows directions ... and is led on a path. A sage carries a compass ... and discovers his own path."

"That's very wise," Shak responded. "You're very wise."

"No, mostly I'm very old," Uncle Josh laughed, "and

wisdom doesn't necessarily come with age. Age comes with age. Wisdom comes from a little bit of knowledge, a little bit of understanding, and I'm sorry to say, often with a whole lot of apologies.

"In my opinion, wise words are snatched from little whispers from God passing through. I try to pay close attention to Him when He grabs my attention. If I say something wise, it's probably because He caught my ear. My only wisdom is knowing that if I want Him to listen to me, I should surely listen to Him."

"Do you think God really listens to us?" Shak asked, with anticipation.

"Most of us don't even understand ourselves, much less anything about Him," Uncle Josh shrugged. "But to be honest, I have my doubts. Considering all the questions and requests that all of creation asks of Him, I wouldn't be surprised if He didn't just allow everything to play out through some normal or natural course of events. Perhaps that is the only way we learn.

"That doesn't stop me from questioning, requesting, and giving thanks, though. I never really know for sure whether I've been heard or answered. But I'm a rabbi. So I talk, and I hope that someone listens.

"The important thing when you speak or question is to listen to yourself. When you do either, you should hear your heart. The difference between a follower and a sage is that a follower is still seeking without, while a sage has found what he was seeking within. We can learn some things about ourselves from without. But we can only truly know ourselves from within."

"Wow!" Shak exclaimed. "Again, that is so wise. I don't even know what to say."

"That's probably because, as usual, I have said too much," Uncle Josh lamented. A wise man speaks because he has something to say. A fool speaks because he has to say something."

"Not at all, Sir," Shak rushed to explain. "I know you are wise because, for the first time, I actually heard what is being said, instead of just trying to remember or memorize some sort of rule or practice to live by. Wisdom really does come with sage.

"I once had a teacher who said that ministers who take the New Testament literally are merely feeding Christians to the lines. I thought it was just a pun. Now I understand the wisdom behind it. You have taught me that the truth is as much within as without.

"That's a lot to think about, and I'm not exactly sure what to do with all of it yet. So, I hope you will allow me the opportunity to discuss this further when I sort it all out in my head."

"You will find that I live for such opportunities," Uncle Josh laughed. "But don't take too long. Neither of us is getting any younger."

It wasn't until much later that Surdas realized that neither Dad nor he had muttered a single word during the entire conversation. It was as though something important had just taken place in all their lives, and like Shak, they were all trying to sort it out. Before that could happen, however, Mother called everyone back to the table for an amazing array of desserts.

Shak seemed decidedly different the rest of the night. It was as though some sort of peace had finally come over him. He was more comfortable in his conversations with John and me, joked a bit with Chip, playfully teased Cayenne into a closer friendship, spared no compliments with Mother and the aunts, all the while remaining amazingly attentive to Surdas, and never leaving his side. Surdas wasn't sure where this trip was leading, but he was certainly enjoying the ride.

When it came time for Cayenne and Shak to leave, Shak put his arm around Surdas, and he had Surdas escort him through each goodbye and thank you. When he finally reached Aunt Sue, he laughed, "The answer to your question is Super!"

"Super what, Baby?" Aunt Sue asked, a little perplexed.

"You asked me what type of sexual I was. I'd say the answer is Super! Like most super people, I just keep it hidden beneath the mild-mannered clothes."

"Well, you know what they say, Baby," Aunt Sue laughed. "You may be super and more powerful than a locomotive, but when it comes to sex, just make sure that you're not faster than a speeding bullet."

"What does all that even mean?" an obviously aroused Surdas whispered, as he escorted Shak to John's car for a ride home.

"That, my friend, is for me to know and for you to someday find out."

Throughout most of that night, Surdas thought about finding out what Shak meant, and he had the second wet dream of his life.

Twenty

The next night, Surdas Zoomed Chris to tell him that, based on Shak's super sexual remark, and maybe partly on his dream, he was fairly sure that he and Shak were finally going to have sex. Chris seemed more than a little surprised. As much as he tried to be somewhat supportive, he was actually far more concerned than Surdas would have liked.

"I know we're guys, and guys tend to take sex a lot more casually than most girls," Chris began, as though on unsure footing. "But this is your first time, and you're still only fourteen. You may not feel like it, but you're still young. There are some things you should know and talk about before your first time. The thought of having sex may be exciting, but it's not a game. I'm not trying to be funny by saying that you shouldn't go into this blindly.

"The thought may seem exciting, but are you sure this is one of those experiences you'll want to remember for the rest of your life? Because you will remember it. You will always remember your first time. So, you'll want to make it something special, something memorable."

Surdas wanted to tell him that he sounded like Mother, but he thought better of it. However, he did pause Chris by responding, "Outside of you, Shak is the only person I've ever met that would be able to make any experience memorable—and you blew it ... well ... actually, you didn't. That's why we're having this conversation now."

"Very funny, Bronco!" Chris replied. (Surdas loves it when he calls him Bronco.) "But I'm serious. You're growing up too fast. Don't be in such a hurry. You're not going to like the grown-up world so much once you get there. There's a lot more sense in innocence than you can imagine."

"I appreciate what you're trying to do, Chris," Surdas replied. "Really, I do! But I also really believe that if I don't do this, I will regret it for the rest of my life. I live with enough shadows without adding another one."

"I don't want to be The Ghost of Chances Lost, Bronco," Chris responded thoughtfully. "Nor do I want to cast any shadows over any bright spots in your life. So, I'm not going to try to talk you out of it. I just want to make sure that you're okay and safe! It's important to all of us who love you that you know what you're doing, and you're careful and safe.

"You know how much I care about you. And I trust you to make the right decision about who the other person is. But I want you to promise me, as one best friend to another, that you'll at least understand what you're doing before you start doing it."

"I have to admit I'm pretty nervous," Surdas confessed. "I was hoping you could give me a few pointers."

"I'm afraid this one is pretty much out of my league, Buddy. I have a feeling you need more advice than just use a condom, relax, and enjoy each other. You should get more expert advice."

"You mean my parents?"

"Hell No! That's way too embarrassing. And rightly or wrongly, they will definitely talk you out of it. No, you need the person that our parents and I turned to when we thought the time was right. You need Mother."

So now, Surdas knew why Chris sounded so much like Mother at the beginning of their conversation. He had experienced the Motherlode before. It appeared that's where everyone went mining for information.

"But won't Mother try to talk me out of it too?" Surdas asked worriedly.

"Of course!" Chris responded. "That's Mother's nature. He wouldn't be Mother if he didn't worry about you. But during the conversation, he will also tell you everything you need to know in case you don't listen. That's also Mother's nature. It's a Mother Knows Best thing, and it's kind of a win-win no matter what you decide."

"Thanks, Chris! I knew I could count on you." Surdas said sincerely.

"Always, Bronco! Always!"

"You know what is also always, Chris? You! … No.1 … in my heart … always!"

"Same here, Buddy! Love ya."

"Love you too, Chris! You are always my first love. I'll never forget that."

"Stop it! You're making me blush," Chris gushed, with a warmth Surdas could feel.

"I know. I actually felt that one coming as I said it," Surdas laughed.

Twenty-One

John and I had plans with some friends the next evening, and Surdas was scheduled to have dinner at Mother's house, so he thought it would be the best opportunity for the whole "the birds and the bees" discussion he promised Chris he would have with Mother. Since dinner at Mother's meant dinner with the entire family, Surdas had to wait an eternity to be able to speak to Mother alone. He seized the opportunity of helping to clear the dishes to get Mother alone in the kitchen to strike.

"Can I talk to you about something a little embarrassing?" he asked, while handing Mother a pile of dishes.

"I've been around these kitchen conversations way too long not to see that one coming, Sweetie," Mother said, with what seemed like an anxious laugh. "Let me guess. Chris told you to talk to me."

"How did you know?" Surdas asked incredulously.

"Let's just say a half dozen of these conversations over the years, knowing how you feel about Shak, and watching you anxiously waiting for dinner to be over, was all I needed to know that something was brewing. I can usually feel the breeze before the storm hits, and you were anxiously playing twister all night."

"I know you're going to tell us to wait," Surdas began. "And I'm sure you'll have good reasons why we should. But Shak may be leaving sometime soon to be with his parents, and we don't know when, or if, we'll ever see each other again. We really care about each other … more than I can ever truly tell you. And it's important for both of us to have something very special to hold on to. Do you know what I mean?"

"Yeah, I do, Sweetie. Probably more than you will ever know. We all grow up too fast, only to be sorry when we get there. And you're right. I'm going to tell you to wait until you're older, so I can tell your parents that I told you to wait until you're older. Because that's what we all think you should do. Then I'll tell you, off the record, of course, the things you should know when you are older, should an opportunity in the distant future arise. And, as I'm sure Chris indicated, I'll leave it to you to determine how far in the future that distant future is.

"Now, I'm sure you've heard this before, but I'm going to tell it to you again anyway because it really is important to remember. Your first time only happens once. You will never have the chance to make it special and memorable again. It's your one shot at a 'Once Upon a Time' opportunity. So, make sure that it's the right time with the right person you want to remember it with.

"I know you boys really care for each other, and you want something special to remember each other by. But the best sex, the most meaningful sex, is about love. It's not a memento. You can do a selfie for that. And by that, I hope you know I mean a photo.

"When you make love to somebody you truly love, there are unspoken words of passion and affection that can never be taken from you and that you will never forget. It is that love, that feeling, you will want to remember—not just the sex.

"Sex, in itself, may seem exciting, but without love, it's just an orgasm. It may be pleasurable; it may even be thrilling; but it's never worth a trip down Memory Lane. And Sweetie, those are the only trips really worth taking.

"I know. When I was young, I made the mistake of taking sex much too lightly, and none of my early experiences were ever memorable. I've always regretted it. It would have been wonderful to have something magical to look back on. Instead, until I met Dad, I mean Tom, all I really had to remember were experiences that were actually forgettable.

"Magic—is incredible. It's something we all long for, and hope to find in each other. That's what your first time should be about—magic, so wonderful that you can't believe it's true.

"Having said all that, I'll say that if I've given you too much to think about, I'm glad. Perhaps you weren't ready. If I haven't, then perhaps I'm the one who isn't ready. Either way, I hope that you and Shak do what's best for the both of you, and you will always be happy with the decision you made."

"You're not going to mention anything to my parents, are you?" Surdas asked worriedly. "That would be rather embarrassing and uncomfortable, to say the least."

"I'll be honest with you, Sweetie," Mother said affectionately. "Your parents and I have discussed the possibility of this conversation way before it happened … just like Chris's parents and I discussed the possibility before my conversation with him. They all understood the difficulties of talking to your parents, and they entrusted me with the responsibility of surrogate should the situation arise.

"I promise you that our conversation, actually all such conversations, will remain strictly private. But I owe it to them to tell them that we talked should they ask. And they, like Chris's parents, are aware and have agreed that's all I will tell them.

"I'm sure I don't need to tell you that you have wonderful parents whose main concern is your concern. They would love for you to be able to talk to them about anything on your mind, but they understand that it's not always easy. So, what's most important to them is that you are comfortable enough to be able to talk to someone who both you and they trust … someone who will always have your best interest at heart. And I hope you know by now that your best interest is always in my heart.

"Now that I've given you the obligatory parental notice, we can settle down to the talk you really want to have, and that I hope you don't need until you are at least thirty-five.

Because, even then, you're still going to be my baby, and I won't be ready."

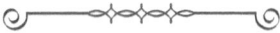

Twenty-Two

S hak and Surdas spent a lot of time with each other over the next several days, although, as Surdas would later confess, there was nothing to dream home about. Shak was attentive, sweet, and everything you might hope for in a great friend; but he was still just a friend, not a boyfriend. And Surdas was afraid he had read too much into Shak's remarks to push matters any further.

During their nightly conversations, Chris thought Surdas was probably just getting ahead of himself, and he suggested that Surdas should just let nature take its course. "When the time is right you will both know it, and Nature will naturally step in. Until then, you are just going to drive yourself and everyone else crazy pushing for the right time."

"How did *you* know when the time was right?" Surdas asked sincerely.

"Just between two best friends," he answered honestly,

"I can't tell you that, because it hasn't happened yet. And it probably won't happen until Molly and I are married."

"Is that a truthful answer … or a mind your own business, you little twit, answer?" Surdas asked, somewhat surprised.

"I told you that I would never lie to you, Bronco," Chris said honestly. "And I meant it. Molly is a headstrong girl who knows exactly what she wants. I'm just happy to be a part of that. She wants us both to finish our education and get good jobs before we get married and settle down. It is her dream that the right time will be when that happens. The right time has to be a two-person decision, and I would do anything to make her dreams come true.

"So, I learned to settle down, because I love and respect her too much to do anything else."

"But doesn't it ever get hard?" Surdas asked, not realizing the double entendre.

"Let's just leave it at Yes!" Chris laughed. "And change the subject back to you pushing for something that may not be the right time."

"But how will I know it is the right time?"

"The only thing I can tell you is that when it's the right time, you will know it," Chris said, with a smile in his voice. "I'm on the outside looking in. All I can see, from my vantage point, are two very confused young guys who may, or may not, think they know what they're doing. Just remember that raging hormones don't think.

"Maybe you need to understand and respect more of each other's plans and dreams before you really know.

Maybe there are a whole lot of maybes that you're both not sure of. I don't know. All I know is that no one else can tell you. And when it's right, you will know.

"I wish I could give you a better answer than that. But I can't. Only you can do that. I can only wish that whatever the answer is, it makes you happy."

"You make me happy," Surdas said, with a smile in his voice. "So, it's always the right answer."

The next morning Surdas still felt confused about the right time, because despite Chris's honest answers and advice, hormones aside, there was still something raging inside him thinking that it might be the right time. He tried calling Cayenne a few times to get another perspective, but he kept getting Cayenne's voicemail. He was about to give up and try calling Chip when the doorbell rang.

Dale and Lauren stopped by to drop off a few souvenirs from their honeymoon in Provincetown. John and I weren't home, and Surdas was feeling a bit desperate, so he built up his courage and asked them if he could talk to them.

"You've always had my heart, Sweetie," Dale replied. "So why wouldn't I give you my ear? And I know Lauren feels the same way. Right, Laur?"

"As a matter of fact," she replied, "we were talking on the way back about how we wish the baby would be just like you." And then laughingly added, "Except maybe a little younger."

"Thanks!" Surdas said, a bit anxiously. "I'm kind of

nervous asking you about this. And I hope you don't think I'm being too stupid."

"But you want to ask us something about sex," Dale said gently.

"How did you know?" Surdas asked, somewhat amazed.

"Because you're a teenager who is way too confident to be nervous and way too brilliant to be stupid," Dale laughed. "So, the only thing that could make a boy like you feel nervous and stupid is talking about sex. I don't know how good we'll be at giving a teenage boy advice about sex, but I promise you we'll give it our best shot."

"I take it this is all about your friend Shak," Lauren added, with a caring, yet knowing tone in her voice. "Don't ask how we know. It's family, so word gets around."

"So, relax and be comfortable, and ask or say anything you want, Sweetie," Dale said kindly. "Whatever you say or ask is just between the three of us and never leaves this room. No one, not even Uncle Chip, will know we talked. So, be as free and open as you need to be."

"Shak keeps making these little references like he wants to have sex with me, but he hasn't made any moves to indicate that he really does. I'm pretty sure that I'm ready to do it. But since he's a little older, and sighted, and a little more forward, or whatever you want to call it, I keep waiting for him to make the first move. I embarrassed myself when we first met by thinking he was flirting with me when he wasn't. Now I'm afraid that I'll embarrass myself again if I'm reading too much into his intimations."

"We won't push it anymore than this," Lauren began,

"but you have to know that both your Aunt Dale and I think you're still too young to be worrying about this. Even your Uncle Chip, who was in his goth period at your age, was probably a year or two away from those concerns. But, having said that, there were other kids our age who were at least claiming to be sexually active. So, the best advice I can give you is to listen carefully to what your Aunt Dale has to say."

"Thanks a lot, Laur," Dale said somewhat sarcastically. "I thought for a second you were going somewhere with that.

"I hope you know how much we love you and want nothing but the best for you," Dale continued, turning her attention to Surdas. "We want you to be happy, whatever course that takes. So, I'm going to skip over the whole waiting thing and tell you to do what's right for you.

"But I will also tell you that you will never know what is right for you unless you are as brave and forthright with Shak as you have been with us. Find out how he really feels. Tell him how you feel. Ask him what, if any, intentions he has. Only then will you know what is right for you. Only then will you know if all your concerns are something to be concerned about. As Mother would probably say, you'll never know until you know.

"If Shak truly cares about you the way you care about him, he will respond one way or the other, lovingly. So, outside of a little disappointment, which you apparently already have, you really don't have anything to lose.

"If he doesn't respond the way you had hoped, perhaps

he just isn't ready yet. You need to respect his feelings just as much as you want him to respect yours. There is nothing more precious than the truth between people who care for each other … even when it hurts. If this is truly an affair of the heart, you need to be able to talk heart to heart. That's where love comes in. That's what love is all about."

"Thank you both," Surdas said, a bit teary-eyed as he hugged them. "I don't think anyone could have given me better advice. That's sure going to be one lucky baby."

"I don't think they will run to their parents any more than you ran to yours," Dale laughed. "No matter how wonderful parents are, and yours are certainly wonderful, it's just the nature of things. I just hope that our kids are smart enough to run to wise old cousin Surdas when they need advice."

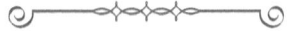

Twenty-Three

Before Surdas had the opportunity to put any of the good advice his aunts gave him about Shak into practice, he finally heard back from Cayenne. And when he did, Cayenne told him a story that so completely outtrumped his concerns with Shak that they never even came up in the conversation.

It seems that Cayenne was hanging around the school courtyard after classes to revel in his newfound popularity. A lot of the other students waved and yelled "Hi!" and "Good Job!" as they passed by. That alone was new and exciting. But about a half dozen of them sat down with him to hear his version of the story, which Surdas was sure grew ever more exciting with each retelling.

Halfway through telling his version of the story, Seth passed by. None of the boys had seen him since the incident with Shak and Surdas in the school hallway. As he passed by, he caught Cayenne's eye and gave a surprisingly shy smile and a quick, simple wave.

Normal Vision?

Cayenne thought Seth looked more than a little lost as he turned to leave. After a few short steps, he turned back around and looked as if he wanted to say something. He stared sadly for just a second or two, and he either had second thoughts about it, or he was dissuaded by the hostile stares from Cayenne's audience.

Cayenne didn't think much about it at the time and hung out with his newfound friends for another hour before heading home. Fame can be fleeting, and Cayenne wanted to enjoy as much of it as he could while the fleet was still in.

A few blocks from home, Cayenne turned a corner and saw someone lying on the ground being kicked and punched by three kids who appeared older and much stronger than their victim. He knew he couldn't possibly handle one of them, let alone three. So he did the only thing he could think of, which was to pretend that he was waving a whole group of friends to join him while yelling, "Hey everyone, hurry over here. Our friend needs our help. Hurry!"

The ruse worked, and the three older kids ran off leaving their curled-up victim behind. When Cayenne reached the boy who took the beating, he was surprised to find that Seth was the curled pile of rubble.

Seth was bloodied and badly beaten, and his shirt was practically in shreds. He stared at Cayenne in absolute amazement through eyes already starting to swell, as Cayenne immediately started silently bandaging Seth's wounds with pieces of his torn shirt.

"What are you doing? I don't understand," Seth said, somewhat dazed through the pain. "Why are you helping me? Why did you save me from those guys?"

"Well, I have to admit that I didn't know it was you when I bluffed those guys away," Cayenne responded. "But it wouldn't have made any difference. I would have done it anyway. Now hold still while I bandage you. You're enough of a mess without making me one too."

"You don't have to do this," Seth grimaced through the pain.

"Oh yes I do," Cayenne smiled. "If you could see what you look like Baby—I mean Seth, you'd realize that I could be charged with leaving the scene of an accident if I didn't clean you up a bit."

Even though his lower lip was also swollen and blood-ied, the comment made Seth smile a real smile. It was the first time Cayenne ever remembered him doing so.

"But why are you being so nice to me?" Seth asked, almost teary-eyed, "Especially after the way I treated you. We both know what a jerk I've been. I don't get it. I would have thought that you would want to get in a few kicks yourself."

"You don't know me very well if that's how you think I get my kicks, Sweetie … I mean Seth," Cayenne responded with a smile. "You may have had a problem with me, but I never had a problem with you. So, there's no reason not to be nice and helpful. It's what good people do. Now quit moving around so much or I'll look as bloodied as you do. People will start to think that I spend my days going around beating up other people."

"Funny! You know, I really wanted to tell you how sorry I was when I saw you with your friends earlier, but I kind of chickened out," Seth admitted, as Cayenne carefully helped him to his feet. "I really am sorry, more than I can ever say.

"I've been thinking a lot about what your friend Surdas and that karate guy said, and I had to confess to myself that they were right. I kept making others pay for an anger that had nothing to do with them. I never really had a problem with you, or your friend, or with anyone else for that matter. The truth is that I had a problem with me, because I had other problems that I couldn't deal with."

"You mean the problem with your dad … and all the beatings?"

"You know about that?" Seth asked, quite surprised.

"I'm afraid everyone does, Sweetie—I mean Seth," Cayenne responded frankly. "You'll have to excuse me. This whole butching-it-up thing is new to me. But anyway, it's a small town, and no matter how you tried to hide them, the beatings were evident most of the time. When it comes to telltale signs, the eyes have it, especially when they're blackened.

"But let's not talk about it now. The outside wounds must be painful enough. Let's get you cleaned up first, then we can talk about the inside wounds if you want. I live just down the street with my grandmother."

"I'm really OK. You don't have to …" Seth started to say before he stumbled and realized how badly he actually felt.

"Yes, I do," Cayenne responded. "You're not exactly a vision of loveliness. You're a mess. And you'd probably scare anyone who saw you all disheveled, hunched over, and slouching toward them. It would be like the zombie apocalypse, or Quasimodo lives again."

"Who?" Seth asked, still somewhat dazed.

"Quasimodo, the Hunchback of Notre Dame," Cayenne laughed. "Surely the name rings a bell."

"You really are kind of funny," Seth smiled, as he tried to laugh through the pain.

"Probably in more ways than one," Cayenne admitted. "But I try to do the best I can with what I've got. I guess that's the best anyone can do. Why were those guys beating you up anyway?"

"I suppose it's kind of a funny story," he replied through the pain, "or at least it's ironic.

"One of the guys said I was staring at him and called me a faggot. So I said, 'You're the one with the frilly shirt and the two boy toys. So, tell me who's the faggot?'

"The next thing I knew I was on the ground, and they were beating the crap out of me. I guess I still haven't learned to keep my stupid mouth shut. It's embarrassing just how embarrassing I can be. Kind of karmic, though, that they beat me up because they thought I was gay, don't you think?"

"And were you?" Cayenne asked coyly. "Staring at him, I mean."

"I don't think so," Seth said sheepishly, "at least not on purpose. Anyway, can I tell you how sorry I am about the way I treated you? I had been so angry for so long that it wasn't until after the altercation with your friends that I realized I had become someone I never wanted to be. I had become my father ... the very person who made me so angry. It made me hate myself as much as I hated him. I have to tell you, it's pretty devastating when you finally realize that you're not worth anything to anybody."

"Everybody is worth something to somebody," Cayenne said seriously. "You just have to find the right somebody."

"Maybe," Seth responded sadly. "But anyway, when I finally took a look in the mirror and realized what a jerk I've been, I hid out in my attic for a few days. I couldn't face anyone—including myself. I don't know how easy it will be not to be the person you never wanted to be. But I knew I needed to figure it out. And I'm certainly going to try."

"You're already that person," Cayenne assured him. "Just by everything you're saying now, and by allowing yourself to feel vulnerable, you're a different person. Can't you see that?"

"Thanks! I'm not sure of anything right now. But again, I need to begin by telling you how very, very sorry I am."

"You already have," Cayenne smiled, "in more ways than you can imagine. Now hush before my eyes start looking like yours."

As Cayenne and Seth got to Cayenne's grandmother's

house, Cayenne warned Seth that the reception inside may be a little chilly. His grandmother had never been very happy with him, so they would just stay long enough to get Seth cleaned up, and then he would help him home.

"Has anyone ever told you that you're absolutely amazing?" Seth asked, as they walked through the front door.

"Amazing, my foot," the imposing figure of Cayenne's grandmother screeched as they entered, and she stared down Seth. "I can't get him to take the trash out, but I see he has no trouble bringing it in."

"This is my friend, Seth, Grandma," Cayenne explained softly, trying to defuse the situation. He got into a little scuffle, and we're just going to clean him up and be gone."

"It figures that would be the type of friend you'd find," she scoffed. "I'm sure it's 'any pig in a poke' for you both. When you're no good, what else are you going to be but up to no good? I don't need to hear any excuses from a couple of poor excuses. Just make sure you clean up after yourselves when you're done.

"And don't go using any of my good towels. The cleaning towels are good enough for the likes of you. And clean them up too when you're done. You're enough of a mess without having to clean one up after you."

"Wow! I think she's tougher than my father," Seth laughed, as she left and Cayenne continued to clean and bandage his wounds.

"You have no idea," Cayenne shrugged. "There are more ways to be beaten than being hit, and she's quite the torture expert when it comes to verbal abuse. The scars don't always show on the outside, but believe me, they're there."

"I guess we have a few things in common," Seth smiled.

"Who would have guessed?" Cayenne laughed. "Wait here while I run upstairs. I have this plain white shirt that I used to wear to church that I think should fit you. You'll be much more presentable in it on the way home, and I don't need it anymore, since presentable in church is something that I'm apparently not. And, apparently to everyone's delight, especially my embarrassed grandmother's, I don't go anymore."

"By the way, what's that stuff you put on my wounds?" Seth asked, as Cayenne got up to fetch the shirt. "It smells kind of nice."

"It is a mixture of aloe, manuka honey, and chamomile," Cayenne said with a beam. "It was a sample at the department store. I'm not sure the whole jar was supposed to be a sample. The instructions weren't very clear."

"Oh! So, you do have a dark side," Seth grinned.

"All my sides are dark, Sweetie. I'm black," Cayenne laughed. The inside, however, is solid gold ... or at least gold-plated. Unfortunately, most people never get past the outside. And I don't even mean the black part."

"You mean jerks like me," Seth said sadly.

"Not just you, Baby. Like just about everyone," Cayenne responded honestly. Being the male version of a femme fatale can be close to fatal."

"You know, I wasn't always a bad guy," Seth said, as

much as to convince himself as Cayenne. "I think I was pretty happy when I was little, and my mom was alive."

"I don't think you were ever a bad guy," Cayenne replied. "I think you were just wounded. All wounded creatures strike out. It's part of Nature. We're no different from any other creature. We're part of Nature too. Nobody thinks straight, if you'll pardon the expression, when they're really hurting. You were never bad, you were just hurting.

"Now, come on. I'll walk you home to make sure you don't get into any more trouble that I have to rescue you from."

"Again, very funny. This may seem weird, considering everything that's happened, and I don't blame you if you say no. But can I buy you a cup of coffee or something on the way back to my place?" Seth asked, while putting on the clean shirt.

"A peace offering?" Cayenne questioned. "And don't say a make-up offer, Mr. Estee Lauder, because you don't have to make up for something that is not your fault."

"Maybe something a little more like an, I'm sorry for being such a jerk and not seeing you for who you really are, offer, and everything else that goes with it," Seth responded. Or maybe even something like a, since you're a special somebody, and I don't have someone like that in my life, can we start all over and be friends, offer?"

"That sounds like a big cup of coffee," Cayenne laughed. "And you don't have to sweeten it any more than you already have."

"Would you mind having a friend who isn't gay?" Seth asked, quite unsure of himself.

"Not as long as you don't mind having a friend who may not be interested one way or the other," Cayenne chuckled.

"You know that people will say that you're kind of scraping the bottom of the barrel if you have me as a friend," Seth confessed in all honesty.

"I may have to scrape you off the floor," Cayenne laughed, "but I would hardly be scraping the bottom of any barrel. Besides, anything at the bottom of a barrel floats to the top if you pour in enough of the milk of human kindness. So, there's no problem. I carry enough containers with me to keep you afloat for a long time. Pretty soon people will be referring to you as the crème de la crème."

"You're really smart and really cool," Seth said sincerely, as they hobbled down the street and into the café where Cayenne and Surdas had recently been accosted. "I truly would like for us to be friends. As you can probably imagine, what I said before is true. I really don't have any."

"I may have seemed a bit popular today," Cayenne chuckled, "but if we become friends, that will double the number I actually have. It will be you and Surdas. So, I'm pretty sure there's enough space on my social calendar to squeeze you in."

"Surdas ... that's another huge apology I have to make," Seth lamented, as the image of their last encounter came to mind. "That poor guy must really hate me. What kind of idiot picks on a blind kid? Actually, what kind of idiot picks on anyone? I can only hope that he's as forgiving as you and at least gives me the chance to try and apologize."

"Are you kidding?" Cayenne assured him. "If Surdas's heart was any bigger, he'd be inside it instead of the other way around. He's so forgiving, he'll probably wind up apologizing to you before it's over. But if it will make you feel any better, I'll pave the way for you before you cross that bridge … or as his grandfather, Mother says, 'Bridge that cross before you get to it.'"

"Thanks! You really are, or hopefully at least will be, a good friend, if you'll have me as one," Seth said hopefully.

"I know this is kind of sudden," he continued, "and it may not be your thing, but I'm going to the basketball game tomorrow, and I'd appreciate your company.

"It's free, so it's my treat," he laughed. "Do you think it's something you might want to do?"

"Basketball? Cayenne chuckled. "That's my favorite of all the balls. It's the big round one, right? The one with the guys with shorts and baskets. Count me in."

"Thanks! I have a feeling this unexpected friendship is going to be a ball," Seth smiled.

"I hope so," Cayenne laughed, "because it will probably be the only ball that this Cinderella will understand."

"You know, thanks to you, I think that I'm beginning to learn how to smile again," Seth said with a huge, albeit painful, smile."

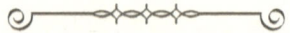

Twenty-Four

The next day, true to his word, Seth kept his basketball date with Cayenne, only, despite the fact that he tried to hide it, he was beaten even worse than after Cayenne had patched him up and left him. It was then that the true friendship began for Cayenne, and he decided to try to find some way to stop the beatings and to never leave Seth alone and vulnerable again.

During the course of their conversation in the café the previous night, Cayenne discovered that, even though Seth was in the same classes as he and Surdas, he was actually two years older than them. He was in the same class because he was left back twice due to poor grades and attitude problems. At sixteen, he was old enough to leave home, but he had neither a place to go nor the money to afford a place of his own. Somehow, Cayenne was going to change that.

After the game, the boys went to the local diner, just down the street from the café, for a couple of orders of fries and sodas. They shared stories and school gossip for at least three hours. Cayenne was impressed with how real and personable Seth could be when he wasn't afraid to not be Seth. When it came time to head for home, Cayenne drew on his inner drag queen and forcefully stated, "You know you're not going home to another one of those beatings, right?"

"Where am I going to go Cayenne?" Seth lamented. "There is no friend's or relative's home to stay in. I haven't the money for anything of my own. There's not even a shelter in this town. I have one option and that's to try and sneak into my house and avoid my father, who's probably drunk and looking for any excuse for an argument."

"No, you have another option," Cayenne stated frankly. "You can sneak into my room in the basement and be safe for once in your life. You can stay there until we figure something else out. We just have to avoid my grandmother the way you have to avoid your father. She should be a bit easier because she goes to bed early on the top floor and doesn't know what time I come in. Actually, she doesn't even care if I do come in. And, just to be safe, I always leave a window open. So, we can avoid the first floor and sneak in that way."

"I don't really think that's a good idea," Seth responded honestly. "I like you and all, but—"

"If you're thinking what I think you're thinking, you'd better get over yourself, and go back to thinking straight," Cayenne snapped. "Right now, you look more like something you'd sweep under the rug than someone who could sweep someone off their feet. So, you're more than safe. I'm just channeling my inner Mother Theresa, and it isn't easy. It's not the best look for someone with drag queen aspirations.

"But, seriously, Baby … and by the way, you're going to have to get used to the whole Baby, Honey, Sweetie thing if you're going to get used to me … I don't know where you're eventually going to live, but I'm going to do my best to make sure that you're at least going to live. That's what friends do. So, if you can deal with a live-and-let-live friendship, we have a deal."

"Have I told you yet how amazing you are?" Seth responded, as his eyes moistened. "I don't recall ever being called anything that didn't have an expletive in front of it. So, being called anything that is meant to be sweet or endearing brings tears to my eyes. As far as the living situation goes, knowing what little I know about your grandmother, you're the one taking the bigger risk.

"If you're sure, and willing to take the risk, maybe we could try it for a day or two and see how it goes. Do you have a place where I can sleep?"

"There's some sort of shag carpet on the floor and an old couch," Cayenne laughed. "I'm not sure which is lumpier, but I'm sure that we can work something out. Maybe you can fit some of your lumps into the ones on the couch and rest there comfortably.

"There's also a bathroom and shower in the basement. Just make sure you don't make any unnecessary noises or leave until I tell you it's safe. We may even have to sneak you in and out of that back window anytime my grand ogre is around."

That night, it probably wasn't the most comfortable situation that Seth found himself in, but he slept better than he had in years. The next morning, Cayenne had to sneak him out the back window as he had warned, and then they sneaked into Seth's home to gather up as many of his belongings as possible. They were just about ready to leave, when Seth's father burst into his room, saw the belongings, and demanded, "What the hell do you think you're doing?"

Cayenne, who was nosing around the kitchen at the time, heard Seth nervously reply, "Look, Dad, I don't want any trouble. I just want out. I'm leaving."

"Where are you going to go, you little piece of shit?" his father demanded, as he pushed him down on the bed. "Nobody wants a worthless bum like you."

"Give me a break," Seth sniffled. "You're calling me a piece of shit? Who do you think is the reason anyone thinks that about either of us?"

"I'll give you a break all right. Do you prefer your arm or your jaw, you ungrateful little turd?" And, just as his father raised his hand to strike him, his hand was met with a large painful strike from a kitchen frying pan.

The shock and the pain brought Seth's father to his knees. And as he clutched the injured hand, he screamed, "Who and what the fuck are you?"

"Your worst nightmare," Cayenne yelled back defiantly.

"No shit, Sherlock!" Seth's father continued to scream.

"You'd be anybody's worst nightmare. I am going to beat the living crap out of you, you little faggot."

But before he could even think about getting off his knees, Seth kicked him over on his side and said, "If you had a shred of decency in your body, which you don't, you'd recognize what decency looks like." And then grabbing his stuff he added, "We are so out of here."

As they headed out the door, with Cayenne still clutching the frying pan, just in case another swing was necessary, Seth's father yelled, "I knew you were a faggot. You've always been a cowardly little faggot."

"I should be so lucky," Seth yelled, giving his father the middle finger. "Instead, I became a bullying lowlife just like you. I don't know if you can change, but you're a great example of why I need to. Fortunately, I have the perfect friend to help me do so. In the meantime, maybe you can beat yourself up for a change. Maybe you'll learn something."

As they started back to his grandmother's house, Cayenne giggled, "At least you'll have a frying pan when we find you a place to live."

"How about—*we'll* at least have a frying pan when *we* find a place to live?" Seth asked sincerely. "You need a decent place to live as badly as I do. I'm sure that you have as many scars on the inside as I have on the outside. And I need a really good guy around to teach me all this really good guy stuff."

"Are you sure you know what you're doing and understand who you're doing it with?" Cayenne responded. "Do you realize that I'm black, Hispanic, and decidedly gay? It's kind of everything you're not."

"Maybe that's exactly the reason it's a good idea," Seth said with a smile. "If you were never happy with who or what you were, why not try something different? The last thing I would want would be to live with someone like me. I just left that."

"You mean you just left someone like you were," Cayenne corrected. "You are not that person now. And, as a matter of fact, you never really were that person. None of this would be happening now if that was the case.

"But I seriously want you to stop and think about it. This is all happening so fast. People will talk if we live together … and they'll make up all sorts of stories about us. And I can almost guarantee from past experience that, at least behind your back, they'll start calling you all kinds of slurs."

"Do you really think they could call me anything worse than the things my father calls me?" Seth assured him. "And if it ever gets to the point where I can't defend myself, at least I'll have you to patch me up again."

"Well, I just might have to go for a medical degree if this is going to work," Cayenne said, with a huge grin, "But I really hope you know what you're saying. Because if you do, I think you just made me an offer I can't refuse."

"Good," Seth laughed. "Because I was hoping that I just made you an offer you couldn't refuse."

Twenty-Five

S urdas was so hung up on Shak, that he didn't even realize it was more than a week since he heard from Cayenne, and that Cayenne was living this whole double life adventure that Surdas knew nothing about. They were making plans for the four of them to finally get together when Shak suddenly insisted on taking Surdas back to the lake so they could once again sit on the overhang of the falls. Surdas could tell by the tone of Shak's voice that he seemed troubled, and so the trip felt clouded by some strange shadow hanging over what should have been a wonderful excursion.

When they arrived at the lake, they freed themselves of their sandals and began climbing the cliff as they had done before. Shak seemed to press into Surdas more than he had on their previous excursion. He did nothing to hide his excitement and even nuzzled into the back of Surdas's neck a few times on the climb up.

Surdas probably would have passed out from the excitement if he didn't sense that the cloud was still there blocking what should have been a ray of sunshine. When they reached the overhang, and were about to sit down, Shak startled Surdas by reaching over and gently running his finger across Surdas's lips and then gently kissed them.

"I have something to tell you," he said. "And it's pretty hard."

"Why do I get the feeling that it has nothing to do with the way you felt pressing against me?" Surdas asked, somehow sensing another dream slipping away.

"In a way, it does," he whispered in Surdas's ear with a hotness that made his knees weaken. "But you're right. I do have some difficult news to tell you. Do you remember how I told you that I would only be here until my parents sent for me? Well, I'm afraid that they have. And I only have a short time left."

This time Surdas's knees did more than just weaken, they buckled; and, as they gave out, he slipped from Shak's grasp and slumped into a crouching position on the overhang. He didn't know what to say. He wasn't even sure if he still had a voice. He just wanted to cry, but he somehow fought it. He just melted into the stone he was crouching on and became part of it.

"Please don't be upset. I didn't know how else to tell you," Shak said, after a few uncomfortable seconds. "That's why I wanted to tell you in a place that was special to us. I hope you understand that this isn't my idea, and I'm going to miss you as much as I hope you're going to miss me."

"I not just going to miss you," Surdas blurted out, finally finding his voice. "I will feel lost without you. You've become the brightest light in the dark that otherwise surrounds me. I wait for that light every day.

"You must know how strongly I feel about you," he said, as his eyes started to water and his will to hold back the tears collapsed. "Everyone else seems to know it.

"Chris likes to joke that I'm like a vineyard when I start to whine. So, I'm trying my best not to be a vineyard. But I'm losing the battle ... because I love you. And I don't care how foolish people think it is when guys our age say things like that ... because I know it's true. I love you, and I'm sure that I will always love you.

"More than you will ever know, I will miss you. I'll miss your words, the music of your voice, your laugh, your touch, your warmth, and the scent of your hair and skin when they are close to me. I'll miss the happiness I feel whenever we're together. I'll miss everything about you."

"I love you too," Shak said, suddenly kissing Surdas on the lips again. "I don't want to leave. I especially don't want to leave you. Everything you said holds true for me too. I tried objecting, but my parents had already worked the whole thing out. And I really don't have any other options.

"My grandmother is giving up her home and will be moving into a nearby senior residence, so she won't need me here. And when that happens, I won't have a place to live, nor any kind of support.

"And, as far as school, I'll be able to continue my courses online in Israel, while we all study with a rabbi who is a great teacher of the Kabbalah. My parents apparently have it all worked out.

"So, you see, all the pieces are falling into place, while everything I want is falling to pieces. I'm out of options. I'm like some crazy control freak who is never actually in control of anything.

"And speaking of crazy, I know this is all so sudden and crazy, and it may not be a fair thing to ask since I need to leave, but after listening to Uncle Josh, I finally realized what I really wanted—and it was you. I want to be with you in any and every way possible. You've become the most important person in my life.

"I was thinking of you when I mentioned the super sexual remark to your great-aunt. If anyone could bring me out of the Clark Kent masquerade, and help me understand who I really am, it would be you. The only reason I kept hesitating about carrying things any further was because of our ages and what our families might think.

"But now, now that it appears that we will be separated for a while, all I can think about is that I would be willing to break my chastity vows if it was with you. Then it would be more like honoring some sort of vow than breaking one. Because of you, it would be something so special, so intimate, and so loving that I truly believe it would be heroic, maybe even approach holy.

"And, although I would hope that the holy would still be hotter than hell, it would be absolutely beautiful, because it was with you. And the way I feel about you is absolutely beautiful.

"Am I making any sense?" he asked nervously. "I know I'm rambling, because nothing but you makes any sense to me right now. Are you at all interested in what I'm trying to ask you?"

"Are you joking?" Surdas asked, somewhat regaining his vitality, and becoming both excited and anxious at the prospect. "That's all I could think about since we met. But I have to admit, I've never done anything before ... at least not with anyone else," he continued with a smile. "So, I also must admit that I'm a little nervous.

"Do you mean right here? Now? Aren't you afraid that someone might see us?"

"Whoa, whoa," Shak laughed. "I wasn't thinking here or now. If it is something that you would want, I was hoping for something a little more private, something special for the both of us, maybe somewhere like the privacy of your bedroom where it would feel more romantic, and not the least bit cheesy. Although, if you'd like, we could explore the cheesy some other time. What do you think?"

"I can't believe that I am saying this," Surdas said excitedly, "and I can't believe that it may actually happen, but my parents have plans for most of tomorrow evening with my Uncles Robbie and Mark who are back in town. So, for a few hours, we will have the house to ourselves.

"Mother will be stopping by to check that everything is OK, but he'll be babysitting my uncles' daughter Madeleine at their house, and he's usually incredibly good at giving me space. So, I'm confident everything will work out if we play our cards right."

"Oh! I'm pretty sure we won't be playing cards," Shak said, with a smile that Surdas could actually hear. "But are you sure you're ready for this? I may be pinning a scarlet letter on you."

"Yeah! Like I'm ever going to see it," Surdas laughed. "And we'll see who does the pinning, Mr. Super Sexual."

"I'm glad you're laughing," Shak said seriously. "We may have to be apart from each other for a while, but we can always be a part of each other. We'll Zoom all the time, and I'll even talk sexy to you, so we don't miss the intimacy too much."

"Perhaps we should just talk and not Zoom if you're going to talk sexy to me," Surdas smiled. "Just in case I can't control myself."

"I'll be counting on my ability to make you lose control," Shak laughed.

"Believe me, you've had that ability for quite some time," Surdas responded, returning the laugh.

Twenty-Six

The next evening, John and I had dinner with Robbie and Mark at our favorite restaurant in town. Neither of our dinner companions seemed like themselves. And so, after an uncomfortable hour or so, I finally blurted out, "Look guys, something is obviously troubling you both. We're more than just friends here. Whatever it is, even if we can't help, I think we should talk about it."

"I'm sorry," Robbie apologized. "I don't mean to be so secretive. I just don't know what I'm doing yet. I have all these big plans that nobody seems to want to hear. And so, Mark and I have been talking about my going over everyone's head and announcing my ideas to the media. Everyone, except us, thinks that's a bad idea since there is a good chance that I may be governor in less than two years, and will be able to talk about my plans then when I have more support.

"The trouble is that I'm tired of doing nothing. And the thought of doing it for another two years drives me crazy. Mark's been amazingly supportive, even though my crazy must be driving him crazy too. And it's not like he doesn't have his own career to think about without worrying about mine.

"I've always been a quarterback. Only in Albany, I'm a quarterback without a team. I have wonderful support from my family, but no team players on my side. I guess I just find it so difficult to sit by myself on the bench when there appear to be so many opportunities to get in the game.

"But enough about this. And I hope I haven't spoiled anyone's dinner. It's not like it's anything tragic. It's more like it's confusing. I keep going back and forth on what I should do. I've always been a football player, but now it feels like I'm playing basketball and no one's throwing me the ball."

"I know it sounds trite," I said. "But if there is anything we can do to help, anything at all, just let us know."

"There is nothing that either you or John could possibly say that would sound trite" Robbie responded with a smile. "It's all loving and deeply appreciated. Just say a little prayer that the ball eventually winds up in my court, and I can get back into the game."

Twenty-Seven

Surdas and Shak's plans for their first experience went along rather smoothly. With John and I dining out with Robbie and Mark as planned, and Mother having retired to their home to take care of Madeleine after checking in on the boys, they were finally left to their own devices.

Shak took Surdas's hand as they started up the stairs to his room. Surdas could tell that Shak was as nervous as he was, but he allowed Shak to continue to take the lead, which made it that much more thrilling for Surdas.

Halfway up the stairs, Shak began kissing Surdas and undressing them both. Surdas could feel his body tremble with every article of clothing Shak excitedly removed. By the time they reached the top step, they were both undressed down to their underwear, and Surdas imagined that every step of the staircase must have been strewn with one article of clothing or another. He suggested that they should probably gather them all up in case Mother returned. But Shak intimated that it was probably pointless, since he could tell by the knowing smile on Mother's face during dinner, that he knew what was going to happen, and probably wouldn't be returning anytime soon.

"What makes you so sure?" Surdas asked, shocked and embarrassed.

"That! And the fact that as he left, he looked me straight in the eyes and said, 'Just remember, that's my baby. And I expect you to treat him like he's yours.' So, my educated guess is that we have plenty of time before we need to re-dress the undressed situation."

And then Shak led Surdas into the bedroom where they quickly crawled under the covers, and after a short uncomfortable silence, he gently slipped his body on top of Surdas's. The heat and feeling of his nearly naked body next to Surdas's was more exciting than anything Surdas ever imagined.

At first, they didn't move or speak. The intensity of their first time was so strong, they couldn't do anything. They just lay there for a while awkwardly smiling, their bodies burning, hard and throbbing with excitement. They probably didn't even realize they were still in their underwear. They just knew they had never felt anything like this before.

After what seemed to be some sort of reflection on what was actually happening, Shak finally began kissing Surdas again and rubbing his body ever so gently up against Surdas's. Surdas could feel the intense heat of their bodies scorching from desire.

Shak's kissing was different this time. It was not like

the quick kisses on the way up the stairs. It was the type of long, beautifully passionate kisses that you only give to someone you truly care about … someone you love. These were the kisses dreams and fantasies are made of. Tears immediately started welling in Surdas's eyes and pouring down his cheeks at the absolute beauty and tenderness of it all.

"Are you all right," Shak gently asked, as he lifted his tear-stained face away from Surdas's. "Is it too much? Should we stop?"

"I've never been better," Surdas smiled through the tears. "Chris and Mother both told me that someday someone who felt as strongly about me as I felt about them would kiss me, and I would know the difference. Now I know the difference. They said it would be beautiful and special, and it is. It's everything I imagined it could be, and more."

"They were right," Shak agreed, obviously touched by Surdas's words, while unconsciously continuing to rub up against him. "The kisses, the feel of your body against mine, are as special and beautiful as you are. This is already the most beautiful moment of my life. And I hope that you don't get too upset at me for saying this, but I think that we should keep it that way.

"I think our first time should be even more beautiful and special than this. It should not be a time when we're sneaking in a quick one in your parents' house, because they're away, or in some place that we may later find kind of embarrassing. It should be at a time, and in a place, where we can slowly make love, and explore one another in a setting that is as beautiful as our feelings for each other.

"And that's why, as much as I want to continue to make love to you, as much as I want this, I think that now may not be the right time. There will be a right time, but it's not now. Do you know what I mean? Am I making any sense? Am I upsetting you?"

Shak may have been right and making perfect sense, but he had been rubbing up against Surdas the entire time he was trying to explain how he felt, and there was no time for Surdas's response, at least not a verbal one. Shak had no sooner finished saying that the time should be right when Surdas's body thought it was … and could no longer wait.

The sudden heaving and exhilaration of Surdas's body, succumbing to a long-anticipated passion, was so intense, that as the excitement escaped from more than just his mouth, the sounds and thrusting of the release caused Shak's body to yield just as quickly. The surrender of their bodies could not have been more thrilling had they tried to carry things further.

After a few breathless minutes of staring awestruck at each other, Shak laughed, "Wow! That was breathtaking! And, as I was saying, I think the next time we should wait until the time is right."

And then, turning a bit more serious, he added, "That was absolutely amazing! You are absolutely amazing! The whole experience really was breathtaking, and I still haven't caught mine. But I really do believe the next time should be very special—not that this wasn't. It was all that—and more. But you are such a beautiful soul. I love you, and you deserve more. You deserve romance, and music, and time to explore each other again and again, in surroundings that we and everyone else would be more comfortable with.

"I know it is a little late to say this while we're still coming out of the Twilight Zone, but I have too much respect for your family to disturb their comfort zone any further than we already have. The next time we'll know when it's the right time and place. And I guarantee you that it will be even more beautiful, even more exciting."

"I understand what you're saying, but you're leaving," Surdas started to protest. "And I don't know when, if you'll excuse the expression, I'll see you again."

"You will always see me in your heart," Shak said, with a gentle smile in his voice. "I may be leaving here for a while, but I'm never leaving there. When you give away your heart, you always come back for the best part of you. Whether it's talking to you every night, or finding ways to come back to you, I'm never leaving you. I'll honor that vow stronger than any other."

Surdas relaxed in the solace of Shak's words. They lay there in Surdas's bed, spent and motionless, their briefs and bodies still covered in each other's excitement, and the scent of their exhilaration still hanging in the air. There was so much warmth and comfort in each other's arms that eventually they both fell asleep.

When Shak awoke, he realized that it must be getting late, so he quickly ran to gather the clothes that they left strewn all over the stairs on their way up. As he opened the bedroom door and reached the top step, he was startled to find Mother halfway up the stairs collecting all that they had left behind, and undoubtedly staring at Shak's telltale briefs.

Mother smiled and simply handed the dumbfounded Shak the bundle and said, "Don't worry, Sweetie, I saw nothing. And by that, I don't mean what you have, nor what you're hardly wearing, which is certainly a lot more than nothing … on the have, not wearing part.

"What I'm obviously having trouble trying to say is, as far as we're all concerned, I'm not here yet, so pay me no mind. As a matter of fact, I wasn't even here until you boys came down and joined me in the living room for some freshly made brownies. Not that you need them, but I understand that they're really good for replenishing your energy.

"And please don't be embarrassed. Believe it or not, I was once young too."

When Shak returned to the bedroom and told Surdas what happened, both boys were embarrassed and reluctant to go downstairs. But, as uncomfortable as it could have been, when they joined Mother for the brownies, he acted as though he didn't know about anything prior to their joining him downstairs, and he kept the conversation as light and enjoyable as possible. He was so warm and pleasant, that both boys momentarily forgot that there was anything at all to be embarrassed about, and simply enjoyed the balance of their time together.

After Shak left, and with the scent of sex still all over Surdas and his room, Mother helped him freshen up. When they were done, Mother asked Surdas, "Are you happy?"

Surdas replied, "Outside of Shak having to leave shortly with his parents, I have never been happier."

"That's all that matters. Then I am happy too," Mother said.

Surdas could tell by Mother's demeanor, however, that he was still a bit worried about him. So, Surdas confided in Mother all that had happened and how what happened was pretty much an accident. Shak didn't want to take what they were doing any further out of respect for each other, and their families. He also told Mother how they decided to wait until they knew the time was right before any future attempt. He could tell the revelation made Mother much more relaxed, and that now he really was happy too.

As Surdas got ready for bed, and Mother tenderly kissed his forehead and tucked him in, Mother said, "I can understand why you feel so strongly about Shak, Baby. Just like you, he's an amazing young man with a great concern for all concerned. It's a beautiful quality, especially in one so young.

"As far as his leaving, don't let what might happen in the future ruin your present. The best present is always the one you already have. Don't let it slip away before you even unwrap it.

"And the strange, magical thing about these types of feelings you're experiencing, is that you never know where they are going to take you. Believe in magic, Sweetie, and it will believe in you.

"A wonderful actress, Audry Hepburn, who I once had the pleasure of meeting, said, 'Nothing is impossible, the word itself says I'm possible.' She was right. Everything is possible until you stop believing in it."

And with that, and one more kiss to Surdas's forehead, Mother left. And almost as quickly, Surdas fell asleep, understanding that there had been so much magic in his life already, there was no reason not to believe in a little more.

Twenty-Eight

Surdas didn't know it at the time, but while he and Shak were planning their first experience, Cayenne and Seth were looking for some sort of part-time work so they could both find a safe and decent place to live, while still secretly sneaking Seth into Cayenne's grandmother's house. Neither one of them was having much luck with the job search. And the sneaking and sharing food situation was becoming more and more difficult, as Cayenne's grandmother began to notice more and more food disappearing. As is often the case in such cases, just when it seemed like things couldn't get any more difficult, they did.

Apparently, Seth had just come out of the shower in preparation for a job interview when Cayenne's grandmother, who almost never went down to the basement, suddenly burst into Cayenne's room. She heard the water running downstairs while Cayenne was busy in the backyard putting out trash. When she saw Seth, wrapped only in a towel, she screamed, "I knew the devil was at work down here. If you're smart, you'll both get out of my God-fearing home before I come back with my large kitchen knife to send you to the hell where you surely belong."

She was so hysterical and furious that they weren't about to call her bluff and try to explain the situation. So, they crawled out the basement window and waited a few hours for her to calm down. When they returned, the doors were all double locked from the inside, the basement window was boarded up, and all their possessions were thrown out on the front porch in two large trash bags.

Attached to one of the bags was a short note that read, "This is a decent home. Have the decency to never enter it again. If you don't know where to go, remember that tomorrow is trash pickup. I'm sure they'll accommodate you."

So, now they were not only desperate and discouraged, they were also homeless. Not sure where to turn to next, they dragged their belongings down to the local coffee shop to drown their sorrows in caffeine and try to figure out their next step.

Cayenne later admitted that it might not have sounded like the smartest solution, but there aren't too many smart solutions when you're their age, and they could at least afford that one. He was about to call Surdas and ask if there was any way he and our family could help, when, without him having to call and ask, our amazing family answered the call.

There are no coincidences, but just by coincidence,

right after Cayenne and Seth arrived, Dale, Lauren, and Chip stopped in the coffee shop on their way home to their apartments. As they sat at a table, they noticed the boys and invited them to join them at their table. The conversation eventually got around to why Cayenne and Seth were there with a couple of large plastic bags. Upon hearing about the types of beatings Seth was experiencing at home, and the trauma of what subsequently happened at Cayenne's home, they decided to try and step in, or perhaps step up, and help.

The first thing they did was to feed the boys as decent a meal as they could get at the coffee shop and then offered them a place to stay for the night. Cayenne slept on Dale and Lauren's sofa, and Seth slept on Chip's. The next morning, they all met for breakfast at Dale and Lauren's apartment. Dale revealed a complicated, but plausible, solution that she spent half the night working on, and that she thought might just solve their problems if she, Lauren, and Chip could get everyone else to agree.

Anyone who knows my family knows by now that they've never turned their backs on anyone who needed help. That's how we all became family. We all needed help at one time or another, and we all wound up becoming part of Mother and Dad's amazing extended family when that help was freely given. The concern wasn't whether the rest of the family would help. It was how and where Cayenne and Seth would best fit in.

Dale thought the best place on the property where the boys would thrive was the house where Aunt Sue, Aunt

Allie, Uncle Josh, and Uncle Mohammed lived. So, the first thing she did was to call Robbie and Mark, who own all the properties, to see what they thought of her plan, and if they agreed. Since hearts are trump in my family, they were all in if everyone else was.

Next, she put Chip in charge of finding out if Uncle Josh would be open to giving up his room on the same floor as the aunts and moving into Mother and Dad's house, which had the two vacant rooms the twins had moved out of. She thought this would be a no-brainer for Uncle Josh, considering how boisterous the cacophony would get with Cayenne joining the aunt swarm. Then she put Lauren in charge of explaining the whole situation to Mother and Dad and making sure that they would be okay with Uncle Josh moving into their house. This again, she thought would be a no-brainer considering Mother and Dad's hearts and their close friendship and history with Uncle Josh. Finally, she took on the task of convincing Aunt Sue, Aunt Allie, and Uncle Mohammed to let Cayenne and Seth move into their house. It was again a no-brainer because of the aunts' close relationship with Cayenne, and, even more so, because that's who my family is. By that, I mean the loving and generous part, not the no-brain part.

Aunt Sue was particularly touched by Cayenne being locked out of his home. She said, "The same thing happened to me when I was Cayenne's age."

When Dale asked him why he was locked out, Aunt

Sue explained, "Because my father caught me blowing bubbles."

"I don't understand," Dale exclaimed. "That sounds very innocent."

"Probably not as innocent as it sounds," Aunt Sue chuckled, as though reliving the memory. "You see, Bubbles was a clown in the local circus."

Anyway, embarrassing Aunt Sue moments aside, and with all that being settled, everyone, especially Seth, agreed that Cayenne should take Uncle Josh's larger room on the floor with the aunts, and Seth would be more comfortable in the smaller guest room on the top floor next to Uncle Mohammed's room.

In return for room and board, the boys agreed to help with all the chores around the property. Considering that the board part involved Mother's cooking, even a scarecrow would recognize a no-brainer.

As you might expect, the whole plan was readily agreed to. And the only condition that the senior members of the family insisted on, was that they would also give the boys an allowance for what they were sure would be chores well done.

The open hearts that led to both open arms and open alms left both boys in tears. They were desperately hoping for a little charity. They got a generous outpouring and a large dose of faith and hope to go along with it. They had been stepping up to the plate and striking out for most of their young lives under unfavorable house rules. They thought that they were about to strike out again. Instead, the family threw them an easy pitch, and they hit a home run.

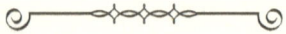

Twenty-Nine

S eth knew Cayenne had paved the way, just as he promised, for the intended apology to Surdas and Shak, by explaining all that had happened before and after Cayenne's rescue of Seth. Cayenne explained how hard Seth was trying to prove that he was a far better person than he appeared to be, and how well he had proved as much already.

Still, Seth insisted, before he could move into the family compound, that he meet with the boys and personally offer his heartfelt apology. Although neither Surdas nor Shak needed the effort, they agreed to the meeting and did their best to make it as easy for Seth as possible.

I have a feeling all the good fortune and kindness, that had come so quickly to a young man who hadn't experienced either for most of his life, was too much for him. Seth collapsed into a hysterical fit of crying halfway through the apology and had to be held by Cayenne and the other two boys before recovering. I imagine that even an abundance of happiness can lead to an overload when you've gone so long without it.

The rest of the introduction of Cayenne and Seth as the newest members of the extended family went as normal as you might expect from a family spearheaded by three retired drag queens with hearts as big as their heels. There was a seamless welcome into the family dynamics by everyone that made the newcomers feel as though they had always been a part of it. There was the fierce "I have your back" sense of security and protection that only a family well-groomed in martial arts, fine arts, and arts not quite so refined can provide. And then there was the traditional family drag queen gauntlet of shopping and grooming that is a once-in-a-lifetime experience, if you're lucky, because the experience usually feels like it lasts a lifetime.

Nothing pleases Mother and Aunts Sue and Allie more than the sprucing up and pruning of the newest members of the family vine, even if the new members are unaware of the necessity. "Appearances may be deceiving," Mother would say, "but the lack of them is deceptively criminal."

Resistance is futile when it comes to the appearance of criminal attire. So the two new perpetrators peacefully surrendered to the fashion police and were carted off to face a trial wherein they had already been convicted and were about to serve their sentence.

Cayenne was the first to surrender and perhaps the most difficult of the pair to clothe. This was not because of any resistance on his part. On the contrary, he was exuberant. It was because of his fluid sexuality. The styles that seemed appropriate and pleasing to the very willing model, and aspiring drag performer, vacillated between the Boys' and the Petite Women's Departments of the clothing store. The shoppers shuffled back and forth so often between the two departments, trying to match outfits, that Aunt Sue asked a very confused store manager to consider a double-crossdresser department with a trans sports section.

Mother thought there was a little too much bling to some of the outfits the aunts helped Cayenne choose. He reasoned that you can still have mod in moderation by accessorizing caution.

"Whatever happened to taste and culture?" he asked Aunt Sue.

"Taste and culture have been relegated to yogurt," Aunt Sue replied. "As Bob Dylan said, '*The Times, They Are A-Changing.*' If you're going to keep up with fashion, you're going to have to be a quick-change artist. Otherwise, you're just a dinosaur loser."

Seth's wardrobe should have been easier since he was far more masculine and basically wore denim. The problem was that the basic denim he wore was just that—basic. That was about to change. His genes were about to go designer. As he tried on numerous pairs of the designer jeans that Aunts Sue and Allie picked out, he finally asked in frustration, "Don't you think they're all just a little too tight?"

"No, I think you are, Honey," Aunt Allie said with a smile. "It's time you loosened up and let the clothes tight-en up. Never be embarrassed when you have nothing to be embarrassed about. You have a body that most people would die for—so let them. Never fight the battle of the bulge when you have one. Let them know that you are packing."

Seth, like all the previous survivors of the shopping gauntlet, gracefully surrendered to what he considered the better judgment of his elders and allowed the fashionista trio to change his appearance from dud to stud.

Surprisingly, he found the change a lot more pleasing than he initially thought he would, as he turned more than a few eyes outside the dressing room while he modeled his new wardrobe. He had experienced so many wonderful changes already, why not go along with another one that seemed to make everyone happy?

With all the wardrobes finally settled, it was on to the shoe department for shoes, sneakers, sandals, and for Cayenne, the aunts' latest drag ingenue … a pair of pumps for practice sessions with Mother and the aunts. As Mother likes to say, "If you're going to be a drag performer, you have to be pumped for it."

The ordeal might seem innocent enough, but the boys still had to endure the squeals in the underwear department—coming, of course, from the aunts, not the boys. The aunts insisted that only briefs would work with the new wardrobes. Considering how brief some of the briefs were, Cayenne was again ecstatic, Seth less so. But at least his weren't as silky as Cayenne's were.

And then finally, the most difficult leg of the gauntlet

… the horrors of the grooming department where manicures, pedicures, and haircuts were in order.

According to Aunt Sue, it took a miracle to have Cayenne's hair dye, which looked like it did, brought back to life, and go from a hair don't to a hairdo. And he swore that Cayenne had to be biting those fingernails and toenails for them to be in the shape they were in. Seth didn't fare much better in Aunt Sue's estimation, as his hair practically had to be mowed, and he needed a blacksmith to have his finger and toe screws chiseled and filed back into nails.

But again, this was all according to Aunt Sue. So there may have been some embellishment in the description of the grooming necessities, especially since he was so disappointed that no one agreed to anything but clear polish on their toe and fingernails. "That's almost like having your bare feet look naked," he bitterly complained, more than once.

After the boys served their sentences in style, the fashion police brought the parolees to the local café, where they were joined by Dad, Surdas, and Shak. The adult table was flooded with descriptions of what a wonderful time everyone had, while the only thing that could be heard above the whispers and giggles at the boys' table was Surdas constantly assuring them, "I know, I know. I've been there. But at least you guys could see what was going on … and off."

"Yes, but at least you didn't have to see everyone else staring at you while it was all going on and off," Seth whispered laughing. "You haven't lived until you see the look on people's faces watching briefs that are too short to be called briefs modeled in front of your crotch."

"Oh yeah, try walking out of the fitting room in pants that are see-through with nothing on underneath," Surdas laughed.

"You did that?" the other three asked, in shocked unison.

"No," Surdas laughed, "but try it."

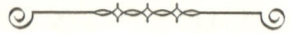

Thirty

When they returned to school, the boys' wardrobe changes did not go unnoticed. Many of the students were amazed at just how cute and stylish Cayenne looked in his cross-dressing mix of young men's and petite women's clothing. And no one was getting more attention than Seth in his new hot, tight, designer look.

All the boys, including Surdas and Shak, who also brought their wardrobes up a notch to match their peers, were starting to get more than a fair share of flirtations from both sexes. They all enjoyed the attention, but their connections to each other were tight, and so, at least in the beginning, no one acted on any of the flirtations.

Strangest of all, the amazing bond that developed between Cayenne and Seth appeared so tight and strong, that it seemed to surprise everyone but them that it never went beyond friendship. But then again, our family has a history of amazing bonds that never went beyond friendship. So, maybe it wasn't really that surprising after all.

Although Seth had never given any indication that he was anything but straight, he certainly appeared infatuated with Cayenne and extremely attentive to his needs. And Cayenne was … well, Cayenne, everything you might expect a blossoming, young drag queen to be. He was bold, loud, a bit self-absorbed, and flirtatious … everything that Seth wasn't. If it's true that opposites attract, there was certainly a lot of magnetism to be found in their relationship.

The two boys appeared to spend every waking moment together, helping with each other's chores, studying, walking to and from school, and sharing in each other's favorite recreational activities. They were inseparable. And the outward appearance gave every indication they were a couple. Therefore, it came as quite a surprise when another student from one of their classes asked Cayenne out on a date, and he accepted.

No one was more surprised than Seth. He was beside himself with jealousy and didn't know what to do. He and Cayenne had become so close. They loved the time they spent together. The date made no sense to him. It was so wrong, so confusing. Why would Cayenne do such a thing?

Since he didn't know what to do, Seth did what everyone else in the family would naturally do in a confusing situation. He sought Mother's advice.

"The first question you have to ask yourself," Mother said, after Seth explained the situation, "is why, if you two boys are just friends, does Cayenne's date with another boy upset you so much? Friendships shouldn't exclude each other from exploring romantic interests outside the friendship. Unless, of course, there is more to the friendship than you're willing to admit. And if there is, you should be honest with yourself and talk to Cayenne about it. If there isn't, you should be honest with yourself and admit that you are being selfish, and allow Cayenne the opportunity to explore a different type of relationship that might be important to him. Either way, it's time to be honest with yourself."

"It's so confusing," Seth responded. "I don't think of myself as gay, I don't think about other guys, yet the only person I want to be with is Cayenne. He's become the most important person in my life. I can't even imagine my life without him."

"Maybe you have to stop putting a label on your feelings and just be honest about them," Mother said. "If you have strong feelings for him, let him know. It may be just what he needs to hear. Trust your heart. Your brain may confuse you with what other people think and say, but your heart will always speak the truth to you. Live your truth.

"If you can't imagine your life without him, then don't. Imagine your life with him, and be the person he couldn't imagine his life without.

"Everybody, but you two boys, seems to know the way you feel about each other. Maybe it's time for you both to openly talk about what everyone else seems to know.

"Life is full of too many woulda, coulda, shoulda experiences, where fear, or ego, or maybe even just life itself prevents you from doing or saying something that might have changed you forever. Then, as the opportunity slips away, you look back with wonder, or regret, and ask your-self, 'If only?' Take the 'if' out of your life.

"I don't know whether it's true, or if it's some sort of urban, or perhaps urbane, legend, but Sue told me that someone once said to the Buddha, 'I want happiness.' The Buddha said, 'First remove "I," that's Ego. Then re-move "want," that's Desire. See, now you are left with only Happiness.'

"Don't let your fears, ego, and desires keep you from happiness. Life should always be about having the cour-age to enjoy the opportunities that you have now. And, whether they work out or not, to bravely look ahead, never looking behind and regretting that you were the behind that let them slip away."

"I know this sounds like fear, but what if I like him more than he likes me?" Seth asked. "What if he likes me but doesn't feel the same way I do?"

"Would you be any worse off than you are now?" Mother gently responded. "The real question you have to ask yourself is, what are you prepared to do if he does feel the same?"

"I don't know. This isn't going to be easy," Seth respond-ed, as the reality of his dilemma sank in. "It all seemed so easy before."

"I know, Baby," Mother replied, with a warm smile. "Affairs of the heart often aren't easy. Nothing makes you feel more naked than baring both heart and soul. It's as exposed and vulnerable as you can possibly get. Honesty takes courage. The good part is that you've already proven that you have plenty of courage, a strong heart, and a beautiful soul. You have everything to gain and nothing to lose by finding the truth. So, whatever that is, you'll be okay."

"Do you really think so?" Seth asked hopefully. "I've never done anything like this before. I usually keep everything to myself."

"No, I don't just think so ... I know so," Mother said warmly. "Mothers know these things."

"Now I know why everyone always comes to you," Seth said, as he tried to summon the courage to take Mother's advice to heart. "If I'm going to start thinking with my heart, can I begin by giving you a big heart-to-heart thank you hug?"

"I'd be disappointed if you didn't," Mother responded, as he opened his arms to the hug."

"Can we just hold it a little bit longer till I feel better?" Seth asked, as he held onto the hug and his eyes moistened.

"As long as it takes, Baby," Mother responded, "as long as it takes. The beauty of a hug is that there are no time limits."

Thirty-One

Cayenne was in his room getting ready for his date when Seth knocked on his door and asked if he could talk to him.

"Sure, Baby. What's up?" Cayenne asked.

"Why are you going out with this guy?" Seth asked nervously, as he fidgeted around the room.

"What do you mean?" Cayenne answered. "It's just a date. I'm not even sure where we're going or what we're doing.

"You know what's weird about it? I've never been out on a real date before."

"We go out all the time," Seth responded, sounding quite hurt.

"You know what I mean," Cayenne said defensively. "I've never been out with someone with potential romantic interests. It's different. It's not just friends. I think this guy may be interested in me in a more-potential sort of way.

"Do you know what?" Cayenne continued. "I've never

even been kissed. Can you imagine … not even one kiss from someone who liked me? It's like in one of those fairy tales, only this time it's the princess, not the prince, who's the frog."

Seth leaned in and gave Cayenne a quick peck on the cheek. "See, no more frog."

"That's cute, Baby," Cayenne responded. "But I'm serious. I'm talking about someone who wants to sweep me off my feet and make mad, passionate love to me. I'm looking for a bushel, not a peck."

"Like this?" Seth asked, as he picked Cayenne up, placed him on the bed, and began hotly kissing him while removing his clothing.

"Seth, what are you doing?" a shocked Cayenne asked, more than a little surprised. "You know that, at least technically, I'm still a boy, and technically you're not gay."

"Why put labels on things?" Seth responded with a smile, secretly echoing Mother. "But if I need one, maybe my label should just read, 'Property of Cayenne,' because that's how I feel. And all I know is that I need you, and I want you. My life is so much better, because you're in it. And I want to do everything I can to keep you there. I found myself, because I found you. And if I don't know what I'm doing, you can tell me, and I'll do it correctly."

"Oh! I don't think you need any help from me," Cayenne responded, as he willingly succumbed to Seth's passion. "And I really don't care whether or not you know what you're doing as long as you keep doing it."

Seth kept doing it. And at one point, he stopped and

whispered softly in Cayenne's ear, "I feel like I'm a part of you, and you're a part of me. I could stay like this forever."

"You'd look pretty funny walking around with a skinny black teenager hung around your neck," Cayenne said with a laugh.

"I'm serious," Seth said. "It's like we're a part of each other ... like we're one. I want to be a part of you that's never apart from you. You make me whole."

There were at least a dozen wisecracks that flew through Cayenne's head, but he wasn't about to let any of them ruin the moment he had waited for all his life. So, he squelched the type of self-effacing humor that had always shielded him, and he smiled in agreement.

Their repeated lovemaking lasted for a few hours, until at last, as they lay peacefully in each other's arms, Seth realized the time and asked, "Do you think you should let your date know that you're not going to make it?"

"I think he knows that by now," Cayenne responded. "The date was more than two hours ago. I'll call him tomorrow to apologize, and say that I couldn't make it because my boyfriend had other ideas.

"I *can* call you my boyfriend, right? I mean this wasn't just a one-shot deal, was it?"

"It's already been more than one shot," Seth smiled. "And hopefully by now, you know how I feel.

"I know I'm not very good with words that express emotions. I never had the opportunity to express anything loving or positive before. But you're all that and more. You're everything to me. You're the reason I smile when

I get up in the morning and the reason I smile when I go to bed at night. My day is not complete unless you're in it. And when you're not, I can't wait for you to be there. Every day with you is filled with more happiness than my entire life before we met. The 'Property of Cayenne' label has already been tattooed on my heart. I hope that someday you feel the same way."

"For somebody who doesn't think they're very good with words, you sure know how to sweep a boy off his feet," Cayenne said, with tears in his eyes. "That's by far and away the most beautiful thing anyone has ever said to me."

"So, did I? Did I sweep you off your feet?" Seth asked anxiously.

"Baby, you had me from that day when I found you all beaten up by those three guys, and you let me take care of your wounds," Cayenne responded. "The entire time I kept saying to myself, 'I could take care of this guy forever.' I wasn't sure then, how long my forever was going to last; but now it feels like it's actually going to last forever."

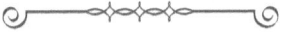

Thirty-Two

The next day, as Surdas was placing his tablet in his locker while waiting for the other boys to arrive, someone suddenly pinned him from behind and removed his wallet. The thief might have gotten away with it if he wasn't so greedy by also trying to remove Surdas's cell phone from a zippered front pocket. As both Surdas and the thief struggled, the perpetrator was suddenly yanked away and sent crashing to the ground in obvious pain. The thief hollered again and again while trying to escape until he finally managed to do so.

"Looks like my hero saved me again," Surdas said, convinced that it was Shak who again came to the rescue, and was relieved that the ordeal was over. "We may just have to replay that bedroom scene over for real this time. But unfortunately, I think he may have gotten away with my wallet."

"This time it's me on the hero end of the scuffle," Seth said, with a knowing smile in his voice that made Surdas shrink. "And I hate to disappoint you, but we probably won't be replaying any bedroom scene. But don't worry, I not only saved your wallet, I also managed to get his. So, now we not only know who he is, we can also report him to the principal."

"It appears that I have quite a few heroes in my life," Surdas responded, more than a bit embarrassed about the bedroom slip. "Thank you for joining the club. I can only hope that it's not going to be a large membership.

"You know what was really strange about the whole thing?" he continued. "The entire time it was happening, he kept repeating, 'I'm sorry. I'm really sorry. I really don't want to do this.' It's weird, but it sounded as if he really meant it."

"That's pretty weird," Seth admitted. "Why don't we just let the principal figure it all out? Unless you want to come clean about the bedroom scene first."

"You can't come clean if you're going to talk dirty," Surdas replied, still embarrassed and trying to laugh it off. "However, I believe there is a secrecy clause in joining the 'Save Surdas Club.'"

"Don't worry," Seth promised. "As a loyal member of the club, the slip is just between us and goes no further. You've been through enough already. The whole bedroom comment will remain under the covers, so to speak."

The boys' trip to the principal's office should have been a happy ending to the story. But the thief, aware that Seth had taken his wallet, tried to beat him to the punch by reporting that Seth accosted him by his locker and stole his wallet. Since Seth had a history of suspensions in the school, the principal took the thief at his word, and when the boys arrived at his office, he had a security officer detain Seth in a separate room while the police were called.

Surdas protested Seth's innocence to no avail. He was told to wait outside the principal's office until the police arrived to straighten things out. Not one to leave anything to chance, he immediately tried to reach John and me by phone, but he was unable to do so. So, fearing that Seth may need some sort of heroic rescue, he called upon the Power Strangers for help. And, almost as quickly as the alarm was sounded, the clouds began to form around the school as Dad rushed Mother and Aunt Sue to the principal's office.

Dad would later swear that the doors to the school and the principal's office blew open as Mother and Aunt Sue stormed through them. As they did, the principal's secretary quickly abandoned her post, and the Riders of the Storm entered the office unannounced. The stunned principal was more than shocked and was already trying to retrieve the papers from his desk that their entrance had scattered all around him.

Mother took a deep breath that probably inhaled most of the oxygen out of the room. He warned the principal, in a tone that even frightened Surdas sitting outside the office, that he had very little time to get this right and save his job, before the town council, the mayor, the lieutenant governor, and the press hear of his inefficiency and inability to maintain a safe environment for the students under his care.

"I'm pretty sure that we got this right," the principal said, almost choking on his lack of confidence. "This boy, Seth, has a history of things like this."

"*Had* a history!" Mother steamed. "He *had* a history of things like this … a history of acting out because you and everyone else on your staff chose to ignore the abuse the boy was experiencing at home. And don't even try to suggest that you didn't know about it. It was abuse that was extremely evident and difficult to ignore. But you all did.

"And now you ignore the fact that the boy has changed and comes to school unscathed, attends classes regularly, has improved his grades, and stays out of trouble.

"Apparently, you are not educated enough to understand that you should never judge anyone by their past when they don't live there anymore. So instead, you decided to be judge, jury, and executioner before hearing any of the facts that might get in the way of an uneducated decision. Apparently being an empty suit suits you just fine, because you have clearly proven that's all you are. Clothes can't make the man when there isn't a real man wearing them.

"And how ironic that your last name is Griffin. I believe that was the last name of the Invisible Man. The difference is, he filled his empty suit far better than you do.

"Well, Mr. Empty Suit, you have evidently heard the fabricated story tailor-made for your convenience," Mother continued, as he summoned Surdas into the room. "Now let's hear the real one from someone who never lies."

As Surdas recounted the incident, the thief started interrupting him by calling him a liar, despite what Mother had said about his never lying. He kept claiming that Surdas was just sticking up for his boyfriend.

"If you don't hold your tongue while my grandnephew is speaking," Aunt Sue finally sneered, in a voice menacing enough to frighten the most hardened of criminals, "I'll hold it for you, you little forked-tongue snake in the class. And, for everyone's information, Seth is not Surdas's boyfriend. If he was, this little rattler would probably be a lot worse off than he is now. But take this as a promise, not a warning. The next interruption you speak will be the last one you will be able to speak for a very long time. And," while turning to address the principal, "that goes for the serpent-tendent of the school too."

After Surdas reported the rest of the story without interruption, Mother demanded that they now bring in Seth to see how closely he could corroborate the story Surdas told.

The principal called the security guard to bring Seth in, and when he arrived, to everyone's alarm, he was handcuffed.

"Hell hath no fury like the fury I'm going to rain down upon your miserable little ass," Aunt Sue screamed at the security guard at the sight of Seth in handcuffs. "Give me the key to those handcuffs, you rusty little tin soldier, before I use them to handcuff your scrotum to the ceiling fan. And if you take the time to take one breath, just one little breath before you do so, it will be your last one. So, save that breath for your quick exit, while there is still a chance that you can make one."

The security guard instantly acquiesced without question and backed out of the room. Aunt Sue released Seth and packed the cuffs and key in his bag with the excuse that they may be needed as evidence—or something.

"Now I understand why you're such a poor excuse for a principal," Mother blared. "What else would you expect from such an unfortunate excuse for a human being? Imagine handcuffing a child when you don't even know the circumstances of what happened. You don't even know the difference between a school and a prison. I imagine that you will be considering handing in your resignation once this is all straightened out. I'd say that you'd be better off as a warden than a principal, if you wouldn't be better suited to be behind the bars rather than in front of them."

"I was as shocked as you at the handcuffs," the principal admitted meekly. "I would never have ordered them. I have no idea why the guard thought it was necessary."

"So, you're saying that you're the lesser of two weevils," Aunt Sue mocked. "Such an admirable defense. I can't even imagine what's restraining me from doing the whole judge, jury, and executioner thing all over your miserable little blockhead and turning that useless appendage into a headstone, you miserable excuse for a miserable excuse."

The principal just sat there frozen at the remarks, as Mother again took charge.

"Seth, take your time, Sweetie, and explain exactly what happened."

Seth's description of the events was as close to Surdas's as possible, considering Surdas is blind and was therefore unable to grasp all the details. As he was finishing, he let slip, "I even gave him …", which he quickly tried to pull back.

"You even gave him what, Baby?" Mother pressed. "It's important that you don't hold back. What did you even give him?"

"I even gave him the chance to tuck back into his sock the bag of weed that slipped out."

"Do you want to show us what's tucked in your socks?" Mother asked the other boy. "Or should we wait for the police to arrive and search you?"

"I'll wait for my parents to arrive before I do anything," he responded nervously.

"That's fine," Mother replied, "but I doubt that the police will be as patient. If you're smart and come clean before they arrive, we may be able to work out a solution that doesn't involve the law and a criminal record."

The boy hesitated for a few minutes as tears began to well in his eyes, and then acquiesced and removed the bag from his sock.

"How about the other sock?" the principal asked, finally finding his voice.

"It's just a cell phone," the boy said sheepishly.

"That's odd," Aunt Sue replied, "since I see another one sticking out of your hip pocket. Perhaps there has been more than one victim in this little crime spree. I think you better hand it over to the principal."

"It belongs to a friend of mine," the boy protested.

"Hand it over, Son," the principal demanded, finally regaining some authority. "We'll see how good a friend we're talking about when we ask the owner."

"I didn't mean for any of this to happen," the boy began to sob. "I panicked. I didn't know what to do. I owed some guys some money for the pot I bought, and they threatened me if I didn't come up with the cash right away. I was afraid to tell anyone, because they said I'd be sorry, and they'd really hurt me if I did.

"I thought I had the money to pay them from birthday gifts from my grandparents, but my parents had taken it and put it in my savings account without me knowing. And I can't even imagine what would happen if I turned to them and explained why I needed it back. I was so afraid and desperate, that I wasn't thinking straight. I didn't know where to turn. I panicked and wound up doing something I never thought I'd do.

"I'm sorry. I was so scared. I swear I'm not this person. I've always tried to be a good guy. I've never done anything like this before. And I'm already in enough trouble without going to jail. My parents are going to kill me, if the guys I owe the money to don't do it first."

"He did apologize a few times while it was happening, and said that he didn't want to do it," Surdas chimed in, feeling sorry for what the boy was going through. "I think he's telling the truth. I think he really meant it. I believe him. He really sounded sorry."

"It's true," Seth added. "Surdas told me as much right after it happened. He kept saying how weird it was that the kid kept apologizing and seemed really sorry that he was doing it."

"OK! I'm going to take you at your word," Mother replied, addressing the boy. "So, you better not be fooling around with Mother's nature.

"This is how it's going to play out. The principal, who is going to get to keep his job and make the halls safer for his students, is going to tell the officers when they arrive that it was all a mistake over a minor scuffle and everything has been settled. He is going to tell the same thing to your parents when they arrive. He's also going to send that very insecure security guard for training on how to properly handle situations involving children.

"In return, you are going to return the cell phone to whoever it belongs to. You are going to apologize to Seth, Surdas, and the other boy for all the trouble you caused. You are going to quit buying drugs and getting yourself in trouble. And you're going to act as hall monitor for the rest of the semester to make sure that no one else in the school gets bullied.

"Do you agree to all of this?"

"Yes!" he cried. "I promise I'll do everything you said. If you can do this, I'll do everything I can to make up for what I've done. I swear that I'm not a bad guy. I'm just a very stupid one."

"Only if you do it again, Baby," Mother said kindly. "Everyone makes mistakes, even serious ones. You're only stupid if you don't learn from them.

"But I want you to remember that you not only came close to ruining your life, you came close to ruining Seth's also. Everything else is forgivable. Ruining someone else's life would not have been. You can't make someone else a victim because you're one. That's when, no matter what the excuse, you become the bad guy."

"And you, Mr. Principal," Mother asked, "do you agree to all that has been said so far?"

"It all sounds like a fair solution," he agreed.

"And exactly how much do you owe these guys?" Mother asked, returning his attention to the boy.

"One hundred and twenty-five dollars," the boy said anxiously, "and I only have twenty of it so far."

"OK!" Mother said, reaching into his wallet, "Here is the balance. You can pay me back by never seeing those guys again, or anyone else like them, and by doing a good deed for every dollar I've given you."

"And do it with interest," Aunt Sue added. "And I mean that in more than one way."

"I don't know why you're being so kind, but I can't begin to thank you enough," the boy sobbed, addressing Mother, and now thoroughly reduced to tears. "You're like some sort of guardian angel that makes everything better. I don't know how I can ever repay you."

"All you need do is live up to your agreements, and

you'll have done enough to repay everyone, including yourself," Mother said softly.

"I will. I promise. I've never done anything like this before, and I never will again. I swear! After all you've done for me, I won't let you down."

"I wouldn't be doing this if I didn't believe you," Mother assured him. "And remember that you would not only be letting me down, but you'd be letting yourself down too."

"You're the most amazing person I've ever met. Can I give you a hug or something?" the boy asked tearfully, unsure of the best way to show how thankful he truly was.

"It's my favorite way to end any situation," Mother smiled. "And I'd say that would be the perfect seal of approval."

"As for you, Mr. Principal," Aunt Sue added, "I hope you've learned that in order to stay on top of things, you have to get to the bottom of them. You're getting off a hell of a lot easier than the boy is. You still have a long way to go before *you* get any hugs.

"You have to learn to walk before you can run. Unless, of course, we have to come back again, in which case you better just run. Maybe the quality of mercy isn't strained, but you're lucky your neck isn't either."

As Mother and Aunt Sue left the principal's office with Dad, Surdas, and Seth in tow, Mother hugged the two boys and told them how proud he was of the way they came to the other boy's defense. "Very few victims would have come to the aid of their offender, no matter what the circumstances. It speaks volumes about your character."

"Speaking of character," Aunt Sue said to Mother, "I knew that somehow you were going to turn that boy around and help him out. Your mind can't even conceive of an ending that isn't a happy one. You're such a softy. You're like that big, gigantic dough boy thing."

"Yet suddenly I'm thinking of popping you in the oven for an ending that isn't so happy," Mother laughed. And speaking of softy, tell me those weren't tears in your eyes toward the end, even though you're Aunt Miss Behaving."

"Allergies," Aunt Sue insisted. "You know how allergic to children I am."

"Hey, you're not allergic to me," Surdas insisted.

"Yeah, well you're about five hundred years old to my way of thinking," Aunt Sue laughed. "So, the allergy to you ended about four hundred and eighty-some-odd years ago. And didn't I see you say something to that boy before we left?"

"Yes. I told him that everyone went way out on a limb for him, so he better live up to his agreements, because I'm going to keep an eye on him. I figured after all he'd been through … he could use a laugh."

Thirty-Three

Our son, Surdas, is exceptional at many different things, but handling emergencies is probably not high on the list.

A few days after the scene in the principal's office, Shak dropped Surdas off at Lauren and Dale's apartment after school to deliver some cookies that Mother made. In the meantime, Shak left to run errands for his grandmother.

Lauren was a few days away from her delivery date, and over the last few weeks, Mother began sending her homemade cookies so that the baby would turn out to be as sweet as his or her mothers. So far, they had kept everyone in the dark as to the baby's sex.

Since Shak wouldn't be back for an hour or so, and Dale was at work, Lauren and Surdas sat down at the kitchen table to enjoy some milk and cookies.

After about ten minutes of family chat, Lauren got up to fetch something and suddenly screamed, "Oh, My God! My water broke."

"You mean your glass of milk?" Surdas asked innocently.

"No, Sweetie! My water! I'm going to have the baby."

"Right Here!" Surdas panicked.

"No! Hopefully not, but soon."

"Do you need a mop or something?"

"No, but I think I need a ride to the hospital. Call Dale, and tell her we are going to have the baby."

Surdas pressed Dale's speed dial number and got her voicemail. So, he just left a "We're going to have a baby," message and immediately hung up.

"Okay," Lauren remarked. "That went well. She's either on the phone or at a meeting. Try Chip."

Surdas pressed Chip's number, got his voicemail, and left the same panicked response.

"Okay, let's try a different approach," Lauren said, anxiously getting a little desperate. "Do you think one of your dads might be home?"

"Which one?" Surdas asked, beginning to panic even more.

"I'm really not that choosy, Sweetie, either one."

"I forgot. Bapu Gene had an important meeting at Town Hall with Aunt Dale and Uncle Chip, and Bapu John won't be back from the city until tonight."

"Okay, just try someone else."

"How about Chris or Shak."

"Chris is at college and Shak doesn't drive," Lauren said, growing a little frustrated. "Try Mother or Dad and tell them that I need to be picked up and taken to the hospital."

Surdas hurriedly pressed one of the buttons, got through, gave the message just as Lauren told him, and added, "Hurry, I think she's still leaking."

Lauren could tell by the scream at the other end that Surdas didn't call Mother or Dad. "Who did you get through to?" she asked, worriedly.

"I was nervous, and pressed the wrong button, and called Aunt Sue," he admitted. "But don't worry, they're on the way."

"I can't even imagine what the admitting room is going to look like," Lauren laughed. "Well, at least I'll have an interesting story to tell the baby when he's older."

"It's a boy?" Surdas questioned. "You're going to have a boy?"

"Yes, but it was supposed to be a surprise."

"Don't you think we've had enough surprises?" he asked, still shaken."

"You're probably right," Lauren agreed with a laugh. "Do you see that bag by the door? Can you grab it, and we'll head downstairs?"

"I don't even see the door," Surdas responded, managing a nervous laugh.

"Right! Now who's the one acting confused?" Lauren asked, as she tried to hurry Surdas along. "I'll tell you what. I'll lead you to the door. You grab the bag. And we'll help each other out to the front of the building and wait for the circus to come to town."

"I'm sorry that I wasn't better at this," Surdas said remorsefully, as they reached the front of the building. "I've never had to deal with any kind of emergency before. I suppose I'm more used to everyone handling them for me. I guess that I'm not quite ready for any kind of crisis hotline yet."

"I think you handled yourself rather admirably, especially considering the circumstances," Lauren responded. "As a matter of fact, I'm hoping that you'll come with me to the hospital, so I'll have some degree of sanity around me until the rest of the posse arrives."

Fortunately for everyone, when the circus did arrive, Mother was the ringmaster in the driver's seat.

All went well the rest of the way, and Benjamin Thomas Poole-Hall, named after Mother and Dad, was born shortly after Dale and Chip arrived.

Although he obviously couldn't see anything, Surdas got to experience his first live birth, hear the baby's first cry, and was given the honor of being the first person, after his birth mother, Dale, and Chip, to hold the baby.

Thirty-Four

After all that happened, Mother's wisdom about not letting the possible future ruin Surdas's present was not wasted on him. There were only two days left before Shak would be gone for God-knows-how-long. The boys weren't about to waste them brooding when they could be enjoying whatever time they had left together. And as Mother promised, there was magic.

As fate would have it, on the first of those two days, Uncle Mohammed returned home from a Ziyarat, or Sufi pilgrimage, visiting the shrines of some of the religion's most important saints, especially that of Jalal al-Din Muhammed Rumi, the founder of the Whirling Dervish order. Shak had never met Uncle Mohammed, and since there was to be a large celebration for his return at his monastery, John and I arranged with Uncle Mohammed to not only get Shak and Surdas an invitation, but also to have Shak take part in the Sema, or whirling ceremony.

Shak was ecstatic. It was one of the few spiritual practices that he had heard much about but had yet to experience. And, from the moment they were introduced, there seemed to be an amazing connection between Uncle Mohammed and Shak. It was almost as though, despite the large difference in their ages, they had always been old friends.

As Surdas and Aunt Allie, who drove the boys to the ceremony, sat on the sidelines, Uncle Mohammed, the semazenbashi, or dance master, introduced Shak to the semazens of the semahane and led him to the center of the ritual hall where he was surrounded by the dancers. He then placed a camel-hair hat on Shak's head and said, "This hat represents the tombstone of your ego. You will now be dressed in a black cloak and a wide white skirt. The white skirt represents the shroud of the ego which will soon be lifted. When you remove the black cloak at the beginning of the Sama, or ceremony, it represents being spiritually reborn to the truth.

"This ceremony is an intelligent and loving ascent to Perfection. By turning toward truth, you will grow through love; transcend the ego; meet and embrace the truth; and arrive at Perfection. You will then return as one who has reached maturity and completion and is able to serve and love all of creation without discrimination. Are you ready to begin that journey?"

With a ring in his voice, Shak responded, "I believe, Dear Uncle, that I have never been more ready in my life."

As the music started playing, Uncle Mohammed instructed Shak to remove his cloak, stand with his arms in a crosswise position, and get ready to experience his rebirth.

"You now represent the number one," Uncle Mohammed explained, "testifying to God's unity with all of creation." He then instructed Shak to open his arms and slowly start revolving from right to left around the heart while embracing all humanity with love.

"Begin slowly. Do not focus on your spinning. Focus only on your journey toward truth. As you pick up the pace to the music, your right arm should be directed toward the sky to receive God's beneficence, and your left hand, in which direction you should be facing, should be pointed toward the earth as you spread God's beneficence to all living creatures. As your pace quickens to the music, your skirt will begin to lift, your ego will be transcended, and your heart and thoughts will meet and embrace the truth on your spiritual journey toward Perfection. You will become one with the One Who is All.

"Now go ... let the music and the chanting carry you ... meet the truth of your perfection ... and His ... and enjoy your most solemn meditation."

Since Surdas obviously could not see the ceremony, but because he had previously partaken in it, Aunt Allie found it easy to describe what was happening and said that Shak appeared to be an angelic center in a swirling circle of white. She said it appeared as though Shak had taken part in the Sama his whole life. So much so, that, unlike Chris and Surdas, he completed the entire ceremony.

When it was over, and he received the congratulations of Uncle Mohammed and all the semazens, there was something different about him. He spoke little of the experience, yet seemed somehow more resolute, more in control.

When Surdas asked him how he felt, he responded, "Like my life is finally going to become my life."

Surdas wanted to ask him exactly what he meant by that, but before he could, Shak said, "I know what you want to know, but you'll have to trust me that, for now, until everything is in place, it is only for me to know." Then he excused himself and apparently went back to talk to Uncle Mohammed again.

Neither Surdas nor Aunt Allie could hear anything that they talked about, but when he returned, Shak was ecstatic and had this beautiful tone in his voice as though something inside him was singing.

Thirty-Five

Later that night, Mother threw a huge festive farewell dinner for Shak with everyone invited including Shak's grandmother. There was celebratory music, celebratory laughter, celebratory non-alcoholic drinks, festive decorations, and three large tables full of every type of food imaginable, all of which were orchestrated by Mother.

Is it any wonder that Kahil Gibran said, "Life doesn't come with a manual, it comes with a mother?" If the perfect manual for a life well lived could ever be written, it would be based on Mother's life.

Before heading to the food tables, Mother asked us all to sit down at the large dinner table so that both John and Uncle Josh could say a few words of thanks for bringing Shak into our lives.

"But first," Mother began, "there is a little surprise … only not for Shak."

And with that, two hands slipped over Surdas's eyes which immediately filled with tears. He knew instantly it was Chris, and he couldn't stop crying for joy. As Chris hugged him from behind, Surdas cried, "Why did you cover my eyes, you big dope? It's not like I was going to see it was you."

"And yet you knew immediately it was me didn't you, you little dope? So, I guess the gesture worked perfectly."

"I can't believe you're actually here," Surdas sobbed. "There's so much I want to tell you, but more importantly there's some people I want you to meet."

"I know," Chris laughed. I've already sized up the competition, and I have to tell you in all honesty, this guy that you like is so good-looking, I'm not even sure if I'm straight anymore."

The remark drew a large round of laughter and quick introductory handshakes from Shak, Cayenne, and Seth, and a hug from Shak's grandmother. After the beautiful words of thanksgiving from John and Uncle Josh, Mother suggested that Shak, as the guest of honor, might also like to say a few words.

"Let us give thanks to All That Is for all that is, and allowing us to share in it," Shak began. "In particular, I'd like to thank all of you for all of this and for sharing yourselves with me. It has been an honor to be a part of the love I have found here and to be able to take so much of it with me when I leave. I know that love will find each one of you wherever you go, because wherever you are, there is love."

After a few hugs, handshakes, and high-fives for the beautiful words, we all headed to the buffet tables, where Chris and Shak took turns piling so much food on Surdas's plate, that he needed help getting it back to the dinner table.

Surdas sat there between the two loves of his life, understanding better than ever what Mother meant about believing in magic, and the best present being the one you already have.

And as he listened to the music of these two loves fast becoming friends and joking about some of the funny experiences that they shared with him, Surdas realized that he had never been happier. And though he knew they would both be gone again soon, he knew he would listen to that symphony for the rest of his life.

As an additional surprise, Cayenne worked up a little drag number with the aunts, featuring a Beyoncé, Rhianna, and Lady Gaga mix. Both Shak and Seth were excited, because they had never seen a drag show before and said they never knew what it was all about.

"Sure you do, Sweeties," Aunt Sue volunteered before leaving to prepare. "Drag is when you dress up pretending to be something that you're not; like old people trying to look younger, young people trying to look older, White people trying to act ghetto, and prejudiced and hateful people going to their houses of worship pretending to be something they're not … loving and decent. The only difference in the drag you're about to experience is that we dress, sing, and act better than all the others. And the only cross we're going to shove in your faces … is in the dressing."

The little show was absolutely amazing. The aunts

framed it to ensure that Cayenne was the star, and he slowly moved from guest to guest singing seductively, as though it was only for them. As he moved toward Shak and Seth, the last two guests to be approached, Surdas couldn't help but think that Seth was either going to freak or faint. But much to his surprise, Chris told him that the only person with a bigger smile on his face than Shak, was Seth. Apparently, his relationship with Cayenne had given birth to a whole new Seth. And, if Chris was right, judging by the way Seth looked at Cayenne as he was being serenaded, the relationship was a lot more intimate than people had imagined.

After a quick change by the performers, and a few more stimulating conversations, Shak excused himself saying he wanted to give Chris and Surdas some time together. As he left, Surdas could tell that the rest of the family also left, giving Chris and him some time alone.

They talked a lot about Shak, how much Surdas was going to miss him, and how much Chris genuinely liked him. When Surdas was sure no one else could hear, he told Chris about the whole premature orgasm ordeal, and how Shak wouldn't take their relationship any further out of respect for their families. Chris laughed about the whole nearly naked Shak and Mother on the staircase fiasco, and Surdas could tell that he was as pleased as Mother to hear about putting things on hold and not doing anything further for a while. Surdas thought that it probably drew Chris even closer to Shak.

And then finally, Surdas asked Chris if he was comfortable with his relationship with Shak. In typical Chris fashion, he responded that nothing would make him happier than to see Surdas happy.

"I can tell that he makes you very happy. So the only catch bigger than the one you get with Shak," Chris said, with a loving smile in his voice, "is the one he gets with you."

"Are you flirting with me, Mrs. Robinson?" Surdas joked.

"Always, Bronco," he laughed, "always."

I'll say it again, Surdas loves it when Chris calls him Bronco. It's as though there is a secret "I Love You" hidden in the nickname every time it's spoken.

After a while, everyone rejoined the boys, and Shak and his grandmother announced they would have to leave since his parents would be arriving early the next morning. Surdas's heart sank as the reality of Shak's leaving began to sink in once again. He was afraid that with Shak's parents' arrival, he might not see him again before he left. Shak promised that would not be the case, and that he would see Surdas the next afternoon with a surprise gift.

As a bonus, Shak arranged with Chris to have a sleepover with Surdas that night so he wouldn't feel as sad or depressed—but only if Chris promised there would be no monkey business with his boyfriend. Chris laughed that it wouldn't be easy, since his boyfriend is definitely some sort of monkey, but he would do his best.

Thirty-Six

Neither Chris nor Surdas got much sleep that night, as their conversations volleyed back and forth over all the particulars, and a few of the intimacies, that you just don't Zoom about. Surdas couldn't believe how wonderful it was to be with him in person again. *I imagine it must be the way I feel when Robbie and I are together.* There is something almost sacred about some bonds, and even when you are developing a very different and more intimate one with someone else, the original bond somehow remains untouched.

There was, of course, no avoiding the subject of Shak leaving in the morning, and it overshadowed even the brightest of topics Chris and Surdas discussed. There was always a warm hug or a strong hand whenever Surdas faltered in being strong. And Chris, much like Mother, was very good at convincing Surdas that if the relationship was meant to be, it was meant to be—and nothing would ever stop it.

"Just look at all the twists and turns this amazing family of ours has flourished through," Chris said reassuringly. "Why should this one be any different? Remember that story of yours about the wizard? Magic doesn't just happen. You make it happen. It happens because that's who you are. Put your inner genie to work."

Still, despite all the wonderful assurances, there was a nagging voice in Surdas's head that kept reminding him, that within a few short hours, the simple touch of two of the most important people in his life would be gone, leaving only the beautiful resonance of their voices. Often what is bittersweet loses the sweet part when you are the one left behind.

Surdas finally fell asleep with the reassuring sound of Chris's voice reminding him of Mother's promise, that if he believed in magic, it would believe in him.

Thirty-Seven

Chris had to leave early the next morning to prepare for a soccer game later that night. So, John, Mother, and I dutifully took up the mission of keeping Surdas's mind occupied throughout the rest of the morning, as he awaited the impending task of saying goodbye to Shak. It wasn't an easy undertaking, but if I say so myself, Surdas has a family of fairly accomplished wizards, so we succeeded far better than I ever would have imagined.

When Shak finally arrived late that afternoon with his parents and grandmother, everyone in my family who was not away was there to greet them. Mother, of course, prepared a late lunch, and after all the introductions and hugs, he invited everyone to come into his home so Shak and Surdas could have a few moments alone together before we ate.

Surdas couldn't even begin to imagine how he was going to say goodbye to the love of his life. But before he could say anything, Shak asked him to come to his parents' car and feel how heavy his suitcases were. Surdas thought it was an odd request, but he didn't care as long as he got to spend a little more time with him.

Surdas agreed that the suitcases weighed a ton, and was further surprised when Shak asked him if he could help move them inside, because they contained a lot of valuable things that he was afraid would be stolen if he left them visible in the car.

"There really is no one else on the property except the family," Surdas mildly protested. "I'm sure everything is safe—and Angel, Mother's dog, would let us know if anyone outside the family came near."

"Still, I would feel much more at ease if we brought them inside," Shak insisted. "It will just take a minute."

Surdas was bewildered, but acquiesced and helped lug Shak's luggage into Mother and Dad's house. When they reached the hall staircase, Shak asked Surdas if he could help him take the suitcases upstairs.

"Why would you want to bring them upstairs?" Surdas asked, absolutely baffled by the way Shak was acting.

"Because that is where my room is," Shak laughed.

"Wait? What? Your room? What do you mean *your room*? What's going on?" Surdas questioned, completely confused. "I don't understand! Your parents are here! Today's the day you're leaving! What do you mean your room?"

Just then, Surdas could hear everyone empty into the hall. And, as Shak gave him a hug, he said with a ring in his voice, "Welcome to my new home … at least temporarily while I finish my studies. I'll be right across the hall from Uncle Josh."

"Wait! What? What in the name of everybody's God is going on?" Surdas exclaimed. "I don't know if someone who is blind can be blindsided, but I think I have been. I'm not sure what's happening, but whatever it is, I'm so happy that it's happening, I'm not even sure I want an explanation in case this dream turns out to be one.

"But then again, I'm finding myself getting terribly excited and happy, and so I just want to make sure that there is a reason to be terribly excited and happy."

"I told you to believe in magic, Sweetie," Mother said from behind, "and it will believe in you. Well, everyone got together to figure out what would be best for everyone. And when that happens, it's magic.

"This started out as Shak's surprise. So, let's all go sit in the living room and let him explain it all to you," he continued, with a huge smile in his voice.

"Well, after the Sema ceremony with Uncle Mohammed, I was convinced that this was where I needed to be," Shak began explaining, after everyone found a comfortable spot in the living room. "I hope you will all forgive me for using familial names in my explanation, as it will make it easier since I will be living here.

"I needed to be near you, and I needed to be near Uncle Mohammed, because I knew in my heart, from the moment I met him, that he was the type of teacher I had been seeking. And I knew that he, with the assistance of Uncle Josh, could help me get past my problem with anger, and find the one thing that I had been looking for all along—the me that I always wanted to be.

"Fortunately for me, Uncle Mohammed more than graciously agreed to let me study with him at the semah-ane, and Uncle Josh agreed to continue our great conver-sations. Add a little bit of Mother's home-spun wisdom and home-cooking into the mix and, for all practical pur-poses, I was accepted into grad school.

"The problem was that there were a lot of problems involved with the decision to stay. I had to convince my parents that this was the right decision. I had to find a place to stay, since I obviously couldn't move in with my grandmother in the senior assisted living residence. I had to find some way of affording whatever place I found. And I wanted to make sure that your parents were okay with our continued relationship if I was able to stay. It was then that the mountain came to Mohammed, and this time I don't mean your uncle.

"With the entire task seeming so daunting, I decided to seek the type of resolution I thought you would seek. So, while you and Chris were talking outside at the Going Away Party, I asked the rest of your family if I could meet with them inside to discuss something extremely import-ant to me. It took all the courage I could muster to do so, considering all the amazing help your entire family had already given Cayenne and Seth.

"I don't think I'd ever been so nervous in my life. Why should this wonderful family stick their necks out even further for someone outside the family that they hardly knew? How would your parents and my parents react when they found out that you were one of the main reasons I needed to stay? There were so many questions and so many reasons why they might consider it to be against their better judgment to get involved. I imagined myself something like Daniel walking into the lions' den.

"Had I known your family better, I might have had Daniel's faith when I expressed my feelings for you and described my predicament. Fortunately for me, as I'm sure you are aware, the den was filled with angels, not lions, and your amazing family immediately started working toward a solution.

"You should probably know that I was very honest with your parents about our relationship, and I promised them, and later my parents, that we would take things very slow, and wait until we were a bit older and wiser to progress any further. I don't think the relationship surprised anyone, but the fact that we intended to take it slow seemed to surprise them, and it eased what might have been a difficult sticking point. I really do believe that everyone understood where we were coming from, and they were just happy for us to be together.

"Anyway, that was addressing just one of the problems. It was Mother's husband, Dad, your grandfather, who came up with the wonderful living solution. With your Uncles Robbie and Mark spending so much time in Albany, and with Chris away at college, there were many chores around such a large piece of property, that the older members were having difficulty with or just not getting to. Dad said since they were thinking of hiring someone anyway, and since there was no one living in Chip's old room, they could offer me a little spending money and room and board for helping out. Apparently, it was the same type of offer they extended to Cayenne and Seth. As you can imagine, with Mother's cooking as part of the package, it was like all of us winning the lottery.

"Now, the only problem left was to persuade my parents. Aunt Sue and Aunt Allie volunteered to try to convince them, but for some reason, the rest of the family decided that may not be the best solution. It was then that your parents, Bapu Gene, and Bapu John stepped up to the plate and hit a grand slam. Who better than parents to talk to parents about their children and their happiness? With the gift of words that only a famous writer and a popular minister could muster, they convinced my parents it would be best for their child to be in a place where he could be truly happy and self-sufficient. It would also be better for my grandmother to have a relative nearby who could help look after her. And, I could even continue to share some of my parents' Kabbalah lessons with them via Zoom, with the help of Uncle Josh, while studying what I felt I really needed to study with Uncle Mohammed.

"Needless to say, your parents are as magical as every other member of your family, and my parents were persuaded to let me stay. But just to make sure that there wouldn't be any last-minute hitches, Aunt Allie and Aunt Sue convinced your Uncle Mohammed to also let my parents partake in a Sema ceremony late this morning. And, with the additional magic that your uncle spun, they came away knowing that they made the right decision.

"As Uncle Mohammed so wisely stated, I now had the roots to ground me, the light of your amazing family to help me grow, and the perfect medium I needed to finally flower into the person I truly want to be, all in one place.

"And that, my friend, is how you became stuck with me as a close-by friend and neighbor, and hopefully one day when we are all ready, something much more."

"No," Surdas cried, as tears of joy ran down his cheeks. "That's how I became stuck with you as another member of the most wonderful extended family in the world. Take it from all of us who are bound together, it's the strongest glue there is."

"After reaching his decision during the Sema ceremony, Shak wanted his decision to be a surprise to you," Mother told Surdas, "just in case everything didn't work out the way he planned. And when it did, he thought telling you this way would be an even better surprise."

"You are going to be so happy living here," Surdas chuckled. "Before you know it, you'll become part of the best-extended family ever. Bapu Gene likes to call it the family vine since so few of us are actually related. I prefer to think of it as a family tree with no branches, but very deep roots. Just wait and see how many times you are going to say this is the best day ever."

"So, is it really the best day ever?" I asked Surdas knowingly, as I wiped away a few tears of joy from my son's eyes. "Have you ever been happier?"

"I'm almost as happy as when my dream of having you and Bapu John as my parents came true," he answered honestly. "I know that they say that you should always count your blessings, but you all fill every day with so many of them that it's impossible to keep count.

"I may not remember to tell each and every one of you, every day, how much I love you. But please know that I do—with all my heart. And if I could count my blessings, the count would begin with each of you.

"I can't wait to tell Chris," he added. "He's going to be so surprised."

"Not as surprised as you're going to be," I laughed, "since he's been watching the whole thing from Bapu John's laptop and was part of the whole surprise."

"Chris, you knew?" Surdas shouted. "And you didn't even give me a hint?"

"I didn't know everything, Bronco," he laughed. "And I certainly didn't want to spoil anyone's surprise. And there were certainly enough of them.

"Let's just say that I went along for the ride with what little I knew, and seeing how happy you are right now, it made the whole trip worthwhile. Besides, it's not like I'd want to miss out on yet another one of your best days ever. As you've told me many times, it's a great way to live your life. And the best part about your best days ever, is that they are always mine too."

"Before I start hugging and kissing you all," Surdas smiled, "including you on the laptop, Cowboy Chris, I have two important questions to ask Bapu Gene and Bapu

John. Do you guys forgive me for not having the courage to confide in you about my relationship with Shak? And are you both okay with our friendship continuing?"

"To the first question," I replied, "all I can say is that there is nothing to forgive, My Son. We understand the reluctance to talk to parents about intimate subjects. We've all been there. We're just happy that you sought good advice. And we just want you to know that we love you and will always be there for you whenever you need us, and even when you don't.

"As to the second question, when we became your parents, the vision that we had was to do whatever we could to make you happy and allow you to continue to become the amazing person we always knew you were. We believe in the person you are, and the person you will become. In many ways, you see things better than we do. We trust in that vision. And if anyone doesn't see that vision as normal, then perhaps they are the ones who are truly blind."

Surdas leaped into John's and my arms hoping to assure us that our wisdom and foresight in the way we helped raise him would not go unrewarded. But, as long as he had already spread his net, he couldn't resist doing a little fishing while he was at it.

"This may just be some sort of wishful thinking on my part." he laughed, testing the waters, or perhaps, slowly reeling in his catch. "But does that mean you trust me enough for Shak to have a sleepover sometimes?"

"Yes," I laughed, "just as long as one of us, or some other adult member of the family is invited too. You may see some things better than we do, but as parents, we probably see things a little differently. Somewhere along the way, I'm sure we will achieve some sort of normal vision."

Thirty-Eight

John and I both thought we had never seen our son happier, or more at peace, than when he said good night to us and went to bed the night that Shak moved in. He fell asleep expecting pleasant dreams about their continued friendship, Benjamin's birth, the addition of Cayenne and Seth, and maybe even his recent experience with Shak. What he found, however, was something quite different.

After a few hours of what he remembers to be a deep sleep, Surdas was awakened by a light so intense that it hurt his eyes when he opened them. Then came the absolute shock of realizing that he was once again seeing light as he did during his near-death experience. As the shock began to ease, and the light started to take form all around him, he found himself once again surrounded by absolute beauty, and in the presence of Lord Krishna.

"I don't understand Lord," he cried, when he once again saw Krishna. "I went to sleep so happy, so peaceful.

I was feeling so good. What happened? Did I ask for too much? Did I somehow die in my sleep?"

"You did not die, My Son," Krishna responded gently. "You are well, and still asleep. Some of this vision you may not even remember in the morning. I trust that some of it, you will.

"Do you remember when we last spoke how I told you that when you live up to your highest potential you are my flute, and you play the most beautiful music the world will ever hear?"

"Of course, Lord! How could I forget?"

"May I ask what that means to you?" Krishna asked.

"Well, Lord," Surdas answered, "I hope to someday be a great writer like Bapu Gene. So, I think if I do that, I would be living up to that potential."

"Ah, hope," Krishna responded with a smile, "is there any dependence, any addiction stronger than hope?"

"I'm not sure what you mean, Lord," Surdas said.

"Hope is a longing or desire for something in the future," Krishna replied. "It is a dream much like this one—a seed that may or may not eventually bear fruit.

"Hope is something you do when you're not actively doing what you should be doing … not being who you want to be. It is like the wishes you make when you blow out the candles on a birthday cake, or see the first star, or throw coins in a fountain. Hope is passive. It is not doing. It is not being. Being is active. Hope is dreaming a life; being is living a dream.

"Wishing doesn't make you who and what you want

to be. Being makes you who and what you want to be. If you truly want to be a great writer, you need to be a great writer. You need to write, not hope that someday you will do it."

"I guess that I have been a bit distracted with my personal life," Surdas confessed, in response. "I know that I haven't written anything in a while, but isn't it also important to experience life and love?"

"Are life and love necessarily distractions from the who and what you want to be?" Krishna asked seriously. "Isn't it possible to have more than one great love in your life at a time? If you love writing, is it really impossible to be a serious writer, and live, and love while you write?"

"I truly love writing, Lord," Surdas responded honestly, "I guess I've been a bit preoccupied with other things for a while."

"Is it possible to love something, yet ignore it?" Krishna questioned further. "Can you be a lover, but ignore your love? Can you be a great writer, but not write?

"That is the difference between being something and hoping for something. A lover loves, a writer writes. As long as you hope to be something, you are not it. There is absolute beauty in doing and being something that you love."

"I understand, Lord. I truly do," Surdas responded, somewhat stunned by the truth that was being revealed to him. "I admit that I was a bit lost. But now that you have once again opened my eyes, I am found. You'll see."

"Let me ask you another question. You said that you

wish to be a great writer like your Bapu Gene. Do you wish to be a writer like your father, or to write like him? There is a big difference. A good writer writes from his own experience, from his own emotions, from his passion. No two souls, no matter how close, no matter how similar, share the same thoughts, the same experience, the same passion.

"If you are to be a great writer, you will never be the great writer that your father is. You will need to be the great writer that you are.

"I know that I have given you much to think about," Krishna continued seriously. "But allow me one more question before I leave you. If I was able to restore your sight and guarantee that your current love would last a lifetime and everything else remained the same, except that you couldn't be a writer, would you make that choice?"

"No Lord, then I wouldn't be me, and I wouldn't be who and what I truly want to be," Surdas responded honestly. "I would love for my relationship to last a lifetime. And I would certainly love to see more of all the wonderous beauty you have already shown me. But I also want to create a beauty of my own. I truly believe that I have a purpose and a talent, and I want to live it."

"Then no more hoping," Krishna said with a smile. "Creating is a process, a conscious intent. Be who and what you want to be. And when you are, share it with a world that needs your gift.

"A person who keeps his gifts to himself is a hoarder. He may think he is wealthy, but the world is poorer for him. A person who shares his gifts is a fountain of wealth, and the world is richer for him.

"You have a beautiful heart, and a beautiful gift, and the world will be poorer if it does not know them. The world depends on people like you to be all that you can be … so that it can be all that it can be, too. You cannot share your gift unless you write. And I cannot fill the world with a beautiful sound without my flute.

"My flute is A Magic Flute, but only when you are the magic behind it. I am ready to hear my flute play. The question is, are you?

"If you are, if you are truly my flute, the writer I believe you to be … then being begins now. If you remember that, when you awake, your inability to see will remain unchanged, but your destiny will be in sight, and you will have perfect vision."

Surdas has remained blind since that night. But he never again lost sight of his dreams. And his perfect vision, as clear and beautiful as anything he ever envisioned, will ultimately be seen in print, and just as clearly, felt in braille.

Conclusion

By now, I think you have a better-than-normal vision of my family and just how exceptional their vision of family is. I trust our hearts and minds have been transparent enough that you have come to love spending time with us, as much as we love spending time with you. Hopefully, you now feel like part of the family. That's how we envision you, so we hope that's how you envision us. Life in the Poole-Hall extended family wouldn't be the same without you.

That being said, let me leave you with another of Mother's insightful sayings to contemplate until we meet again.

"To see is to be aware of something outside of yourself. To envision is to be aware of something inside yourself. Visualize both—and you will be aware of something greater than yourself."

Visualize love; visualize happiness; visualize until your heart's content. Most important of all, without question, visualize the you that you always wanted to be; because, in reality, that's who you really are.

Then, like our son Surdas, you will have better-than-normal vision.

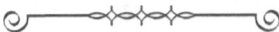

About the Author

Stephen Mulrooney's thirty-something year dream of becoming a writer began to take shape in 2009 when the characters in these books began telling him their stories. It took another three years before he realized the best way to become a writer was to actually sit down and write. It helped. Stephen Mulrooney's critically acclaimed first novel, *Normal?* was the first book in, what has become, the *Normal?* series.

Normal Too? was Steve's second book and the much-anticipated sequel to its predecessor. Apparently, the characters that told Steve their story in the first book haven't stopped talking. He hopes you enjoyed their further adventures in that book as much as he has.

Normal Curve? was Steve's much awaited third novel in what Steve decided to extend into a series. It was ten years since Steve finished the first draft of *Normal Curve?* During most of that time, it sat patiently waiting for our return to it, to cut and polish it into the beautiful gem it became.

Normal Vision? is the latest, and fourth novel in the continuing *Normal?* series. It turns out his characters have much more to say than Steve ever imagined. He hopes you enjoy the ever-increasing Poole-Hall extended family, and their continuing adventures as much as he loves listening to them. By the way, Steve and the entire Poole-Hall family always think of you, dear reader, as one-of-the-family.

Steve still lives in Kansas City, MO with his husband, Jerome P. Van Wert, and their feline family. Tigger, the incredible cat, showed up one day and eventually took up residence.

Stephen J. Mulrooney

Busterfly

Why did I name the company Busterfly?

Our Friend's Story

The name Busterfly is a tribute to our wonderful canine friend, Buster. Buster was a male Neapolitan Mastiff. He came into our lives one cold February evening. If you would like to read the full story, or if you would like to stay up to date with Stephen J. Mulrooney's continued adventures with the *Normal?* series, or meet up with Steve for a book signing, check in every-so-often at the link below.

www.busterfly.com

LOOK FORWARD TO STEPHEN J. MULROONEY'S
NEXT BOOK IN HIS NORMAL? SERIES

NORMAL HEART?

From

Busterfly

a small, personal, fun-loving publishing company